The Sermon of Saint Anthony to the Fish and Other Texts

The Sermon of Saint Anthony to the Fish and Other Texts

António Vieira

Translated by Gregory Rabassa

University of Massachusetts Dartmouth
Dartmouth, Massachusetts

Library of Congress Cataloging-in-Publication Data
Vieira, António, 1608-1697. [Selections. English. 2009]
The sermon of Saint Anthony to the fish and other texts / by Antonio Vieira; translated by
Gregory Rabassa.
    p. cm. – (Adamastor book series) ISBN 978-1-933227-30-6 (alk. paper)
1. Catholic Church–Sermons. 2. Sermons, Portuguese–Translations into English.
3. Prophecies. I. Title.
BX4705.V55S4713 2009
266'.28109032--dc22   2009039474

This publication was made possible in part by a grant from the Luso-American Foundation.

Table of Contents

António Vieira's Empire of Word, Sea, and Sky
Vincent Barletta

In spite of the best efforts of modern researchers, much of António Vieira—whether by this name we refer directly to the man or point metonymically to his extensive and largely performative textual corpus—remains bathed in shadow. This darkness, the work of nearly four centuries of time, the vicissitudes of a life lived as much in Amazonian jungles as in European capitals, and more general problems involving the indeterminate nature of the linguistic sign, is by no means complete. Like a peculiar form of *chiaroscuro,* there do emerge small areas of light from so much shade and uncertainty, as though some piece of Vieira—a kind of authorial or, more accurately, oratorial presence residing latent in the text—were to appear to remind us of our inadequacy before the Word of God and the missionary project of His church.

   The present introduction seeks to play a bit within the few fields of luminescence (as well as within the tense back-and-forth that exists between these and the oceans of darkness where almost nothing can be seen or shown with any certainty) that Vieira affords to us. I will first briefly examine Vieira's very subjective account of the events that took place immediately after his delivery of the "Sermon of Saint Anthony to the Fish" on June 13, 1654; of primary interest to this examination are the complex theories of language and verbal interaction—implicit and yet somehow always present, as if just below the surface—that Vieira develops within the various texts from which this account emerges. Having presented these theories, I will then turn to Fernando Pessoa's foundational twentieth-century reading of Vieira. This modern(ist) Vieira, separated from the light of revelation and Ignatian spirituality, is in many ways the Vieira that we have inherited and continue to engage at the beginning of the twenty-first century, even as we labor now to separate ourselves from the ethical pitfalls of the millenaristic imperial framework within which Pessoa situates his predecessor.

AT SEA WITH WORDS AND THINGS

Three days after delivering his allegorical "Sermon of Saint Anthony to the Fish" to a bewildered and largely hostile audience of colonists assembled in the Igreja da Sé in São Luís do Maranhão, António Vieira set off for Lisbon. Vieira's reasons for undertaking the dangerous sea voyage to Portugal in the summer of 1654 were relatively straightforward: he hoped to gain support at the Bragança court for his proposal to reform dramatically the structure of colonial government in Northern Brazil. A plan to consolidate the two captaincies general of Maranhão into one governorship (the idea being, as Vieira himself phrased it, that one thief would ultimately do less damage than two) was then being discussed, but Vieira had by early 1654 already thrown his weight behind the more revolutionary idea—expressed in the "Saint Anthony" sermon—that the indigenous population, as well as the evangelical mission that for Vieira justified Portuguese imperial expansion in the first place, would be better served if there were no colonial governors at all. He puts this point perhaps most succinctly in a letter to King João IV (1603-56) written on April 4 of that year:

> Here there are men of good quality who can govern more transparently and also with more respect for authority. Even if they do work in their own interest, it is always with a great deal more moderation and, in any case, all of their profits remain here so that this land continues to grow in wealth. Should these men be granted estates, they would receive them as lords and not as leaseholders, as is the case with those that come here from Portugal. But, once the Indians are free from governors and this root—which is the principal and original sin of this province—is pulled up, all of the other sins that proceed from it will also cease, and God will have more reason to grant us mercy. (*Cartas do Brasil* 440)

As was the case with earlier colonial figures such as Fray Bartolomé de las Casas (1484-1566) and Vasco de Quiroga (1470-1565), Vieira's sincere concern for the native population was mitigated only by the limitations of the Christian evangelical framework within which he worked and had been educated. It follows from this that his reference to "original sin" in relation to the structure of colonial government in Northern Brazil should be understood as a complex declaration of both ethical and metaphysical principle. In strictly political terms, it should also not be passed over that Vieira's plan for native self-government at the regional level would effectively put the missionary work of the Jesuits at the very forefront of the Portuguese colonial enterprise in Brazil. As Thomas M. Cohen has argued, "Vieira's criticisms of Portuguese imperial and ecclesiastical institutions were deeply rooted in the pastoral thought of the Society of Jesus in general and of Manuel da Nóbrega, the founder of the Jesuit missions in Brazil, in particular" (2). In closing his April 4 letter to João IV, Vieira goes so far as to make his case for the Jesuits in an explicit and direct manner: "May Your Majesty free us [i.e., the Jesuit missions] once and for all from the petitions and claims of Your Majesty's ministers; because if we are not totally exempt from them, we will never be able to achieve the end for which we came—the conversion and salvation of souls—and it would be better for us to leave and focus solely on the comforting of our own souls" (*Cartas do Brasil* 440).

Whatever may have been the most important underlying motives for his petitions to the ailing Portuguese king (João IV, who suffered from acute gout, would be dead from renal failure less than two years after Vieira's arrival in Lisbon), Vieira set off for Lisbon on June 16 to help put these petitions into effect. He left behind him an extremely tense and dangerous situation in Maranhão, evidenced in large measure by the sharp content of the "Saint Anthony" sermon itself, as well as by his efforts to keep the details of his departure a closely guarded secret.

It took nearly five months for Vieira to cross the Atlantic and arrive in Lisbon. The principal cause for this long delay was a strong oceanic storm that struck Vieira's ship as it approached the Azores. Such storms were a relatively common occurrence in the Atlantic (underscoring the dangerous nature of these crossings and, as a result, the always precarious nature of colonial administration and commerce) and Vieira took the opportunity—in the middle of a sermon on Saint Theresa of Ávila—to convert his brush with death into a full-blown miracle narrative. Leaving implicit in the sermon the winds that were slowly tearing apart his ship and the waves that were by then coming over the gunwale (according to witness accounts, things had become so desperate that Vieira began to offer general absolution to the crew), Vieira describes his prayer to God and the guardian angels of the souls of the unconverted natives of Maranhão:

To whom had it ever happened, after his ship had turned over and everyone had been left hanging onto the broadside, that the ship remained still for the space of a quarter-hour, without the fury of the winds tearing it apart, without the force of the waves swamping it, and without the weight of the cargo and the water—from which the ship was half-submerged—sending it to the bottom? And to whom had it ever happened that after all this the ship should turn over yet again to right itself and allow back in all those that had been thrown outside? The angels of heaven, whose help I called upon at that time, are witnesses to this; and not all the angels, but only those responsible for the souls of the unconverted natives of Maranhão. "Guardian angels of the souls of Maranhão, remember that this vessel is on a mission to bring succor and salvation to those souls. Do now what you can and must do, not for the sake of we who do not deserve it, but for the sake of those helpless souls that are in your charge. Know that they are lost here today with us." I spoke all this in a loud voice that was heard by all those present, and the worthiness of the cause compensated for the indignity of the orator. The angels set to work because God heard the prayer. And God could not help but hear it because it was the danger itself that spoke within it. God knows that no worldly interest, after I had come to know such interest and then leave it behind, would cause me to return to the sea except for the salvation of those poor treasures, each one of which is worth more than infinite worlds. And as the danger was undertaken for love of God and my neighbor, how could there not be security in the midst of so much danger? (Azevedo, *História de António Vieira* 1, 217)

In the end, the guardian angels of the unconverted natives of Maranhão sent along a Dutch pirate ship to rescue Vieira and his shipmates and transport them safely to the Azorean island of Graciosa (what could be saved of the ship's cargo was transported to Holland to be sold). Vieira remained there for two months before proceeding to Terceira and then to São Miguel. On October 24, 1654, Vieira finally set off for Lisbon aboard an English merchant ship along with several other clerics and a cargo comprised mostly of songbirds. The ship passed through a series of tempests on its way to continental Portugal and Vieira, with his usual rhetorical élan, dedicates a section of his "Sermon for the Fifth Sunday of Lent (1655)" to a poetic description of the scene on the ship during these storms: "The birds sang because they lacked understanding; the heretics ridiculed us because they had no faith; and we who had both faith and understanding shouted to the heavens, struck our chests, and cried for our sins" (*António Vieira, O Chrysostomo portuguez* 1, 469).

Vieira's various accounts of the dramatic maritime events that transpired just after his pronouncement of the "Sermon of Saint Anthony to the Fish" are significant in that they reveal many of the dominant features of his work as an author, orator, missionary, and historical figure. The foremost of these has to do with the implicit but by no means unsophisticated theory of language that informs Vieira's words and actions. Throughout his written work, Vieira consistently promotes the idea of a tight and complex correspondence between the verbal utterance and the objects of the world. This idea makes of textual exegesis and the sermon, as well as narrative itself, a practically endless commentary on God's created universe, as António J. Saraiva points out:

> The equivalence between text and thing makes it so that any utterance is but a commentary on the inexhaustible verbal reality constituted by all that exists. For this reason, the term "lexicological discourse" defines skillful discourse very well. In fact, the rules followed by signifiers that do not possess more than a biunivocal relation with their signifieds are, at their core, those that correspond to grammar, lexicology, and rhetoric. Logical relations and those that stem from scientific laws are only applied to signifieds. It is for this reason, as we have seen, that classical discourse presupposes a definite distinction between text and what we call concept or "reality." If this distinction is abolished, what remains are only grammatical relations between words and the sets that they constitute. Commentary is verbal: it is the commentary of that great text to which everything that exists is reduced. For a skillful author such as Father António Vieira, everything is either Word or Speech. But Speech has no boundaries. (*O discurso engenhoso* 89)

Following this line of thought, Vieira's narrative account of the oceanic storms in both his "Sermon on Saint Theresa" and "Sermon for the Fifth Sunday of Lent (1655)" constitute glosses on the *logos* presented at the beginning of the Gospel of John (*en archê ên 'o logos*) and so themselves explicitly possess literal, allegorical, anagogical, and moral levels of meaning. Beyond these more or less traditional Christian modes of interpretation corresponding to what Dante Alighieri describes as "polysemantic" discourse in his letter to Can Grande, Vieira's sermonic narratives of personal experience also possess the much more striking pragmatic capacity to forge relations of contiguity between the verbal sign and the context of utterance. In fact, due to the complex temporal relations that permeate and inform Vieira's theory of verbal discourse (and interaction) with respect to the revealed word and created world of God, these narratives also work to forge relations of contiguity and co-presence with the context of the events recounted.

The wrecked ship at sea, which Josiah Blackmore has singled out as a fundamental trope for the Portuguese Empire during the seventeenth century, becomes for Vieira at once (and the multi-layered simultaneity of this image is a central aspect of his poetics) a commentary on colonial politics, the Counter-Reformation, the Jesuits' missionary project in Brazil, the torment of the human soul, and the role of language and speech within God's created universe. If words and things exist and operate on essentially the same plane for Vieira, it follows—in practice, in any case—that they bleed into one another to fashion a potentially endless and pragmatically charged proliferation of signification and praxis. It is, in fact, the perceived unmooring of rhetorical devices from their scriptural (and thus "real") harbor that so vexes Vieira in his famous "Sermon for Sexagesima," in which he attacks the Dominican preachers of the Portuguese court for their empty rhetorical flourishes. As Alcir Pécora puts it, for Vieira "the detachment of rhetoric from the theological-missionary project presupposed in analogy is intolerable. Absent this decorum and with form granted autonomy outside of reason, the public's applause constitutes a condemnation, given that it celebrates a 'false testimony' of God's word" (19). Such "false testimony" not only drifts off into artificiality but also, at a more basic level, sinfully posits for Vieira the very possibility of a breach between utterance and God's word.

From an anthropological perspective, the theory of verbal interaction that Vieira develops in his "Sermon for Sexagesima," as well as in his "Sermon of Saint Anthony to the Fish" and others texts, provides surprisingly explicit and agentive roles for both speaker and audience (it in fact foregrounds the role of the audience, both piscine and human) and situates the verbal utterance within frameworks that are at once social, contingent, and, perhaps paradoxically, eternal. And all of this would be complex enough were it not also formed out of and developed to work within the settings of violent colonial discourse and practice that were central to the shaping of Vieira's life and work. As much as Vieira's intellect and rhetorical genius pull modern readers in the direction of various forms of decontextualized analysis, such explicitly interactional frameworks serve to remind us that it is ultimately within these settings that we must approach his written work, as well as the active reception of that work during the whole of the seventeenth century.

TWENTIETH-CENTURY TREMBLINGS

Fernando Pessoa, writing in the third cycle of his quasi-epic *Message*, famously effects a strange sort of poetic apotheosis for António Vieira: "Heaven fills the blue with stars and is majestic / He, who had fame and now has glory / Emperor of the Portuguese language / Was to us a heaven as well" (*Mensagem* 108). It should be pointed out that in referring to Vieira as the "Emperor of the Portuguese language" Pessoa is presenting something much deeper than a two-dimensional metaphor of Vieira as the greatest of Portuguese prose writers—a form of poetico-monarchic appel-lation more suited, in any case, to popular musicians and athletes (e.g., Amália Rodrigues as the "Queen of Fado," Vicente "el Rey" Fernández, and George Herman Ruth as the "Sultan of Swat"). For Pessoa, Vieira was not only a great writer but also, in a very concrete sense, the high sovereign of a realm of existential authenticity and sublime—albeit linguistically mediated—reason in which Pessoa (if Bernardo Soares is to be believed) fervently desired permanently to reside. This, we might fairly believe, is much of what Pessoa (as Soares) means when in the *The Book of Dis-quiet* he declares: "My nation [*pátria*] is the Portuguese language" (225). This statement, which has found its way into everything from official state documents to language course syllabi, is no love letter to the Portuguese language (or, *a fortiori*, to Portugal); rather, Pessoa is engaged in the much deeper and more ambitious project of elaborating something analogous to Martin Heidegger's philosophy of language and placing Vieira at the very center of a system of expression, perception, and being-in-the-world. As dramatic and even reductive as such a reading might seem, it is not too much of a stretch to rephrase Pessoa's declaration of linguistic citizenship and Vieira's sovereignty over that domain as a reworking of Heidegger's famous maxim regarding language as the house of being. As Pessoa might have put it: "Language is the house of Being, the Portuguese language is the house of *my* Being, and to that house António Vieira holds the key."

    In speaking of Vieira in this way, Pessoa is in large measure releasing Vieira's own vision of empire—a spiritual, ecumenical, and ultimately uto-pian one, with Portugal at its evangelical center—from its Christian and Neo-Scholastic moorings so that it might float through the darker waters of Pessoa's idiosyncratic modernism. Pessoa's complex re-reading of Vieira's theories regarding the central place of Portugal in what might be under-stood as something like a Catholic caliphate with the missionizing church (and the Jesuits) at its center, a utopian "Fifth Empire" built upon more spiritual grounds than its Assyrian, Persian, Greek, and Roman predecessors, is beyond the scope of this introduction. What does interest us here, however, is the place of Vieira's *oeuvre* within Pessoa's idiosyncratic form of nationalism and what it might mean now for our own readings of Vieira.

In the first place, the basis for Pessoa's posthumous coronation of Vieira is at once reasoned and deeply emotional. In essence, Pessoa invoked and altered Vieira's vision of spiritual empire and rooted it in the only sort of remembrance of things past that mattered to him (at least in his Soaresian avatar): those revolving around language and literature. Writing once again in the *Book of Disquiet,* Pessoa speaks of his first experience with Vieira's prose:

> I weep over nothing that life brings or takes away, but there are pages of prose that have made me cry. I remember, as clearly as what's before my eyes, the night when as a child I read for the first time, in an anthology, Vieira's famous passage on King Solomon: "Solomon built a palace…" And I read all the way to the end, trembling and confused. Then I broke into joyful tears—tears such as no real joy could make me cry, nor any of life's sorrows ever make me shed. That hieratic movement of our clear majestic language, that expression of ideas in inevitable words, like water that flows because there's a slope, that vocalic marvel in which the sounds are ideal colors—all of this instinctively seized me like an overwhelming political emotion. And I cried. Remembering it today, I still cry. Not out of nostalgia for my childhood, which I don't miss, but because of nostalgia for the emotion of that moment, because of a heartfelt regret that I can no longer read for the first time that great symphonic certitude. (224-25)

Pessoa's sadness here is not triggered by Vieira's prose *per se* but rather by his inability ever to return to his first experience of it. In some sense, he has been relegated—through and due to time—to a relation of vicariousness with his own former self and, more tragically, with Vieira's revelational poetics. In a very practical sense, Pessoa continues to have contact with the "symphonic certitude" of Vieira's prose; however, he can only look back through the half-light of his memories to gain access, and then only partial access, to the powerful feelings—and inner movement, as though a key had turned in a lock and a door opened—that this prose first engendered. Like Saint Augustine shaken by the story of the life of Saint Anthony (of Egypt, not Lisbon) or reading himself to Christian conversion in a Milanese garden, Pessoa (once again, as Soares) offers his own sort of conversion narrative, with Vieira—and Vieira's Portuguese prose—at its very center.

Philosophical considerations aside, in playing a poetic Pope Leo III to Vieira's Charlemagne, Pessoa places the seventeenth-century Jesuit priest at the pinnacle of a twentieth-century, openly millenaristic vision of empire built not upon military conquest and dominion, but upon the delicate foundation of the Portuguese language itself. Pessoa by no means developed this vision of Vieira and empire *ex nihilo*. Saraiva has described in great detail the "religious theory of Portuguese worldwide expansion" upon which much of Vieira's writing is based, while also calling attention to the important place that the sixteenth-century poet, cobbler, and would-be Old Testament prophet Gonçalo Annes Bandarra (who, like Vieira, had been brought before the Portuguese Inquisition) has within Vieira's prophetic vision of empire in general ("António Vieira" 32). Many of Vieira's earlier sermons in defense of the Portuguese restoration and the ascension of the Bragança dynasty, in fact, involve a subtle redirection of the messianic discourse of *Sebastianismo* that leaves in place much of the structure of this diffuse and popular movement.

For Anglophone readers in the early twenty-first century, aware of the ominous postcolonial implications of Vieira's evangelical and linguistic vision (Antonio de Nebrija's late fifteenth-century maxim regarding language as the "companion of empire" cannot but ring in our ears), Pessoa's coronation of Vieira can justifiably conjure up a great deal of ambivalence and even Conradian horror. Phillip Rothwell, in a book-length analysis of *lusofonia*, postcolonialism, and nationalism in the novels of the Mozambican novelist Mia Couto, makes this point about Vieira and Pessoa's linguistico-imperial-messianic vision even more directly:

> At the time [Pessoa] was writing, his attitude was remarkably progressive. However, in a postindependence era, his influence on the mindset of lusophone intellectuals becomes highly problematic because language, as Ngugi Wa Thiong'o points out, is one of the principal weapons of neocolonialism. If the language is deemed to be the homeland, a claim is made for metropolitan jurisdiction over the literary output of a diverse set of countries that happen to use the language in the postindependence era. (48)

This statement is not necessarily meant as any sort of indictment of postcolonial organizations such as the Comunidades dos Países de Língua Portuguesa (partial sponsors of the recently constructed Museum of the Portuguese Language in São Paulo), but it does problematize the somewhat romantic notion, even if seemingly liberating in its earliest enunciation, of the Portuguese language as a shared homeland for Africans, Brazilians, and Europeans alike. One imagines, at least, that if the guardian angels of the unconverted natives of Maranhão have any say in the matter, then a much more secure and less subjunctive homeland will find its way into being, at least for the indigenous communities of Northern Brazil. In any case, there can be little doubt that we are due for a renewed appreciation of Vieira's complex but still relevant place within the broader debate regarding the legal rights of the indigenous populations of Brazil and the Americas as a whole.

We would do well, also, to dig deeply into the "symphonic certitude" of Vieira's writing as we strive to understand the processes by which both Portugal and Brazil became independent, if poorly-defined nations (the former from the Habsburg dynasty in 1640 and the latter from Portugal in 1822) and then clawed their way toward modernity. Vieira's sermons echo still through the streets of Lisbon, even if no one but the mercury-addled rockling and cod of the Tagus estuary hear them. And in the Brazilian state of Maranhão, where the indigenous community has been reduced to less than one percent of the total population, Vieira's entire textual output takes on the calamitous tone of Old Testament prophecy. One might say that if it fell to Bartolomé de las Casas simply to make known the atrocities then occurring in Castile's American colonies, it was Vieira's much sadder fate to see the future with his own eyes and, Cassandra-like, have his warnings and visions fall on deaf ears.

Works Cited

Azevedo, J. Lúcio de. *História de António Vieira*. 2 vols. Lisbon: Clássica, 1992. Print.

Blackmore, Josiah. *Manifest Perdition: Shipwreck Narrative and the Disruption of Empire*. Minneapolis: U of Minnesota P, 2002. Print.

Cohen, Thomas M. *The Fire of Tongues: António Vieira and the Missionary Church in Brazil and Portugal*. Stanford: Stanford UP, 1998. Print.

Pécora, Alcir. "Sermões: O modelo sacramental." *António Vieira: Sermões*. Ed. Alcir Pécora. São Paulo: Hedra, 2000. 11-25. Print.

Pessoa, Fernando. *Book of Disquiet*. Ed. and trans. Richard Zenith. New York: Penguin Books, 2003. Print.

———. *Mensagem*. Ed. Caio Gagliardi. São Paulo: Hedra, 2007. Print.

Rothwell, Phillip. *A Postmodern Nationalist: Truth, Orality, and Gender in the Work of Mia Couto*. Lewisburg: Bucknell UP, 2004. Print.

Saraiva, António José. "António Vieira, Menasseh ben Israel et le Cinquième Empire." *Studia*

Rosenthaliana 6 (1972): 25-56. Print.

———. *O discurso engenhoso: Estudos sobre Vieira e outros autores barrocos.* Lisbon: Perspectiva, 1980. Print.

Vieira, Antônio. *Cartas do Brasil.* Ed. João Adolfo Hansen. São Paulo: Hedra, 2003. Print.

———. *António Vieira, O Chrysostomo portuguez: ou, O padre Antonio Vieira da Companhia de Jesus; N'um ensaio de eloquencia compilado dos seus sermões segundo os principios da Oratoria Sagrada.* 2 vols. Ed. Antonio Honorati. Lisbon: Mattos Moreira, 1878. Print.

Sermon of Saint Anthony to the Fish

Preached in São Luís do Maranhão in 1654, three days before embarking secretly for Portugal

Vos estis sal terrae.[1]
Matthew 5:13

I

Speaking to preachers, Christ our Lord says, "You are the salt of the earth," and he calls them salt of the earth because he wants them to do to the earth what salt does. The effect of salt is to impede corruption, but when the earth is seen to be as corrupt as ours is, even with so many on it doing the work of salt, what can the cause of such corruption be? It is because either the salt is not salting or because the earth is not letting itself be salted. Or the salt is not salting because preachers are not preaching the true doctrine; or the earth is not letting itself be salted because the listeners, while the doctrine given them is true, refuse to receive it. Or the salt is not salting because the preachers say one thing and do another; or the earth does not let itself be salted because the listeners would rather imitate what the preachers do than what they say. Or the salt is not salting because the preachers preach for themselves and not for Christ; or the earth is not letting itself be salted because the listeners, instead of serving Christ, serve their appetites. Is all of this true? Unfortunately, it is.

If we assume, then, that either the salt is not salting or the earth is not letting itself be salted, what is to be done with this salt and what is to be done with this earth? As regards what is to be done with the salt that is not salting, Christ said subsequently: *Quod si sal evanuerit, in quo salietur? Ad nihilum valet ultra, nisi ut mittatur foras et conculcetur ab hominibus.*[2] If the salt loses its flavor and effectiveness, and a preacher is lacking in doctrine and example, what must be done is for them to be cast out and to be trodden on by men. Who would have dared to say such a thing if Christ himself had not so declared? Therefore, just as there is no one more worthy of reverence and exaltation than the preacher who teaches what he should and acts accordingly, so also deserving of all scorn and of being trodden underfoot is the one who preaches the opposite either with his words or with his deeds.

This is what is to be done with salt that does not salt. What is to be done, then, with the earth that does not let itself be salted? Christ our Lord does not resolve that point in the Gospel, but we have its resolution from our great Portuguese Saint Anthony, whom we celebrate today together with the most gallant and glorious resolve ever undertaken by any saint.

Saint Anthony was preaching in Italy in the city of Rimini against the numerous heretics there and, since errors of understanding are difficult to uproot, not only were the saint's efforts fruitless, but the people came and rose up against him and were close to taking his life. What would the generous soul of the great Anthony do in that case? Would he shake the dust off his shoes as Christ advises elsewhere? Anthony, with his bare feet, could not have made that protest, however, and feet that have not picked up anything from the earth have nothing to shake off. What was he to do, then? Withdraw? Fall silent? Pretend? Bide his time? That would have been what prudence or human cowardice might teach, but the zeal for divine glory that burned in that breast would not surrender to such expedients. What did he do, then? He simply changed pulpits and listeners, but he did not abandon his doctrine. He left the town squares and went to the beaches; left the land and went to the sea, and he began by saying in a loud voice: Since men do not wish to listen to me, let the fish hear what I say. Oh, wonders of the Almighty! Oh, powers that created land and sea! The waves began to seethe, the fish began to gather, large, middle-sized and small, all arranged according to their kind, with their heads out of the water, and Anthony preached while they listened.

If the Church wants us to preach about Saint Anthony on the Gospels, let them give us someone else. *Vos estis sal terrae*: That is good text for the other holy doctors, but in the case of Saint Anthony it falls quite short. The other holy doctors of the Church were the salt of the earth, Saint Anthony was the salt of the earth and also the salt of the sea. This is the theme I have chosen for today, although for many days now I have had it in my head that on saints' feast days it is better to preach like them than to preach about them. All the more so because the state of my doctrine, whatever it may be, has had in these lands a fate so similar to Saint Anthony's in Rimini that it has become necessary to follow him in everything. I have

preached to you many times in this church and in others, in the morning
and in the afternoon, by day and by night, always with very clear, solid,
true doctrine as it concerns what is most necessary and important in these
lands for the correction and reform of the vices that are corrupting them.
The fruit of this doctrine and whether the earth has taken the salt or has
been taken by it, you know quite well, and I feel sorry for you.

With this in mind today, in imitation of Saint Anthony I wish to turn
from the land to the sea, and since men no longer make use of my words,
I shall preach to the fish. The sea is so close by that they will hear me
quite well. Others can forget about the sermon because it is not for them.
Mary means *Domina maris*, "Mistress of the sea," and since my theme is so
unusual, I hope she will not deny her customary grace. *Ave Maria*.

II

What shall we preach to the fish today, then? No better audience. Fish, at
least, have two good qualities as listeners: they listen and they do not speak.
There is only one thing here that might discourage a preacher, which is
that fish are people who are not going to let themselves be converted, but
that difficulty is so widespread that it is almost no longer felt anymore.
That is why today I shall not be speaking of Heaven or Hell, and, therefore, this sermon will not be as sad as the ones I preach to men when I set
them to remembering those two ends.

Vos estis sal terrae. You must know, brethren fish, that salt, a child of the
sea like you, has two properties that are used on you too: to preserve and
to prevent corruption. These same properties are contained in the preaching of your preacher, Saint Anthony, as they should also be in that of all
preachers. One is to praise good, the other to condemn evil: praising good
in order to preserve it and condemning evil in order to prevent it. Nor
should you think that this is only for men, because it has its place with
fish too. So says that great Doctor of the Church, Saint Basil: *Non carpere
solum, reprehendereque possumus pisces, sed sunt in illis, et quae prosequenda
sunt imitatione*. "It is not only necessary to observe and condemn fish," the
Saint says, "but also to imitate and to praise them." When Christ compared his Church to a fishnet, *Sagenae missae in mare*, he says that fishermen "gathered the good into vessels, but threw the bad away": *Elegerunt
bonos in vasa, malos autem foras miserunt*.[3] And where there are good and
bad it is necessary both to praise and to condemn. With that in mind, in
order for us to proceed in a clear way, I shall divide your sermon into two

parts, fish: in the first I shall praise your virtues, in the second I shall condemn your vices, and in this way we will satisfy the obligations of the salt, for it is better for your to hear it while you are alive than to experience it after you are dead.

Beginning with your praises, then, brethren fish, I could well say that of all living and feeling creatures you were the first that God created. He created you before the fowls of the air, before the beasts of the earth, and before man himself. God gave man rule and dominion over all the animals of the three elements and in the provisions by which he honored him with those powers, the first ones to be named were the fish: *Ut praesit piscibus maris et volatilibus coeli, et bestiis, universaeque terrae.*[4] Of all the animals of the Earth, fish are the greatest in number and in size. How can the number of species of birds and land animals be compared to that of fish? What comparison in size can be made between the elephant and the whale? For that reason, Moses, the chronicler of creation, while not mentioning the names of any other animals, names only the whale with his *Creavit Deus cete grandia.*[5] And the three singers in the furnace of Babylon also sang of him as singular among all others: *Benedicite, cete et omnia quae moventur in aquis, Domino.*[6] These and more praises, these and more excellent qualities of your breed and greatness I could tell you, oh, fish, but leave that for men who let themselves be carried away by such vanities and leave them also for where adulation has a place and not in the pulpit.

Coming to your virtues, then, brethren, which are only worthy of true praise, the first to appear before my eyes today is the obedience with which, when called upon, you all come to honor your Creator and Lord and the order, quiet, and attention with which you listened to the word of God from the mouth of his servant Anthony. Oh, what truly great praise for fish and what a great affront and confusion for men! The men persecuting Anthony wanted to cast him out of the land and even from the Earth, if they could have, because of his condemnation of their vices, because of his refusal to speak the way they wanted him to and to go along with their errors, and, at the same time, the fish, in a gathering beyond count, came to hear his voice, attentive and hanging on his words, listening in silence and with signs of admiration and assent (as if they possessed understanding) to what they did not understand. What was someone to say if he looked at land and sea at that moment and saw men so furious and headstrong on land and fish so quiet and pious in the sea? He might have thought that the irrational fish had been changed into men and the men not into fish but into wild beasts. God gave the use of reason to men and not to fish, but in this case men had reason but no use for it, and fish had the use without the reason.

You are worthy of great praise, oh, fish, for the respect and devotion you have had for preachers of the word of God, all the more so because this was not the only time you had it. Jonah, a preacher of the same God, was traveling on a ship when that great storm arose, and how was it that men treated him and how did the fish treat him? The men threw him into the sea to be eaten by fish and the fish that ate him carried him to the shores of Nineveh so he could preach there and save its people. Can it be possible that fish give aid for men's salvation and men throw the ministers of salvation into the sea? Have a care, fish, and do not boast of how much better you are than men. Men's inner selves made them throw Jonah into the sea and the fish took Jonah into his inner self and bore him alive to land.

But because omnipotence had a greater role than nature in these two actions (as it also has in all the miracles wrought by men), let me pass on to consider your natural and special virtues. Speaking of fish, Aristotle says that only they among all animals have neither been tamed nor domesticated. Among land animals the dog is quite domesticated, the horse quite regulated, the ox quite serviceable, the monkey quite friendly and fawning, and even lions and tigers can be tamed through wiles and benefits. Among animals of the air and excepting those birds raised by us and living with us, the parrot speaks to us, the nightingale sings to us, the falcon helps us and gives us sport, and even the great birds of prey withdraw their talons as they recognize the hand of one who gives them sustenance. Fish, on the other hand, live in their seas and rivers, dive into their depths, hide in their grottoes, and there is none so large that he trusts man or so small that he does not flee from him. Authors generally condemn that characteristic of fish and ascribe it to too little docility or too much brutishness on their part, but I am of quite a different opinion. I do not condemn, rather I have great praise for that withdrawal by fish, and it seems to me that if it were not in their nature, it would be showing great prudence. Oh, fish! The farther removed from men, the better. May the Lord preserve you from any dealings or familiarity with them! If the animals of the land and air wish to be on a familiar footing with them, let them be so all they want for their room and board. The nightingale may sing for men, but in its cage; the parrot may tell them clever things, but chained to its perch; the falcon may go hunting with them, but with its tether; the monkey may clown for them, but on his log; the dog may be happy gnawing on a bone, but led where he does not wish to go on a leash; the ox may take pride in having them say he is handsome or noble, but with a yoke across his neck pulling plows and carts; the horse may glory as he chews on a golden bit, but under whip and spur; and while lions and tigers may feed on a ration of meat that they did not catch in the forest, they are imprisoned and locked up behind iron bars. You fish, however, far removed from men and those social activities, will live along among yourselves, yes, but as fish in the water. You have the example of all this truth from people's houses and everything inside them and I want to remind you of it because there are philosophers who say you have no memory.

In Noah's time the flood came, covering and inundating the world, and of all the animals, who escaped, free from it all? Of the lions, two escaped, a lion and a lioness, and so on with the other land animals. Two eagles escaped, male and female, the same as with other birds. But what about the fish? They all escaped, and not only did all of them escape but they became even more widespread than before because land and sea were all sea. Since all land animals and all birds died in that universal punishment, why did not the fish die too? Do you know why? Saint Ambrose says because the other animals, being more domesticated and closer to men, had more contact with them, while the fish lived far away and removed from them. God could easily have poisoned the waters and killed all the fish, as he did with all the other animals who drowned. You certainly have experienced the strength of those herbs by means of which, when wells and lakes are infested, the water itself kills you, but since the flood was a universal punishment that God visited on men because of their sins and on the world because of the sins of men, it was the lofty providence of divine Justice that there be diversity or distinction in it so that the world itself see that all the evil had come upon it because of the company of men, and that was why the animals who lived closest to them were also punished and those who were far off went free.

See, then, oh, fish, what a great boon it is to be far removed from men. When a great philosopher was asked what was the best land in the world, he answered the most deserted, because men were at farthest remove from it. If Saint Anthony also preached this to you, and if this was one of the benefits for which he exhorted you to give thanks to the Creator, well might he have claimed it, because the more he sought God the farther he fled from men. In order to flee from men he left his parents' home and joined a religious order where he took a vow of perpetual seclusion. And because even there he was not left alone by those he had left behind, first he left Lisbon, then Coimbra, and finally Portugal. In order to flee and hide from men he changed his habit, changed his name, and even changed himself, hiding his great wisdom beneath the appearance of an idiot so that he was neither known nor sought out, but, rather, left alone by all, as happened to his own brothers in the general chapter of Assisi. From there he withdrew to lead a solitary life in a wilderness from which he would never have left had God perforce not given a sign, and he finally came to the end of his life in another desert, all the closer to God for being all the more distant from men.

III

This, oh, fish, is the common nature that I praise in all of you, and the happiness I congratulate you for, not without envy. Getting down to particulars, we would have to cover infinite material in dealing with the virtues that the Author of nature has endowed you with and made admirable in each of you. I shall only make mention of a few. And the one that holds first place among you all, so celebrated in Scripture, is Tobias's holy fish, to whom the sacred text gives no other name but "great," as it truly was in the inner virtues, which are the only elements of true greatness. Tobias was walking along in the company of the angel Raphael and going down to wash the dust of the road off his feet on a river bank when, behold, he was attacked by a great fish whose mouth was open in the act of trying to swallow him. Tobias cried out in fear, but the angel told him to grab the fish by its fin and drag it up on land and to open it up and take out its entrails and keep them, because they would be of great use to him. Tobias did so, and when he asked what virtues did the insides of that fish have for the angel to order him to keep them, the angel replied that the gall was good for curing blindness and the heart was good for driving out demons: *Cordis ejus particulam, si super carbones ponas, fumus ejus extricat omne genus daemoniorum: et fel valet ad ungendos oculos, in quibus fuerit albugo, et sanabuntur.*[7] That was what the angel told him, and that was what experience showed him later, because, as Tobias's father was blind, when his son applied a bit of the gall to his eyes, he recovered his sight completely; and as a demon named Asmodeus had killed Sara's seven husbands, Tobias himself married her, and when he burned part of the heart in the house, the Demon fled and never returned. The gall bladder of that fish gave Tobias the elder back his sight and drove the demons out of the house of Tobias the younger. Who would not have great praise for a fish with such a good heart and such an effective gall bladder? Surely, if that fish had been dressed in a monk's habit with a cord tied around it would have looked like a maritime portrait of Saint Anthony.

Saint Anthony would open his mouth against heretics and come to them carried away by the fervor and zeal of divine faith and glory. And what did they do? They cried out like Tobias and were afraid of that man and thought he wanted to eat them. Oh, men, if only there were an angel who could reveal to you the nature of that man's heart and that gall that embitters you so much and how necessary it is for you! If only you could open that breast and see the insides, how surely you would discover and come to know clearly that there are only two things asked of you and for you: one is to enlighten and cure your blindness and the other to drive the demons from your homes.

So, whom do you follow to cure your blindness, to free you from demons? There was only one difference between Saint Anthony and that fish: the fish opened its mouth against someone who was cleansing himself, and Saint Anthony opened his against those who did not wish to cleanse themselves.

Oh, people of Maranhão, there is so much I could tell you now about this case! Open up, open these innards. Look, see this heart. But, oh yes, I was forgetting! I am not preaching to you, I am preaching to the fish.

Going from the fish of the Scriptures to those of natural history, is there anyone who does not have great praise and admiration for the celebrated virtues of the remora? On the day of a saint of a lesser order, lesser fish must come first before the others. Who is there, I say, that does not admire the virtues of that little fish, so small in body and so great in strength and power who, no larger than the palm of your hand, clings to the rudder of a ship from India in spite of sails and winds and its own weight and size and catches on and clings tighter than the very anchors, preventing the ship from moving or going forward? Oh, if only there were a remora on land that had as much strength as the one in the sea, there would be fewer perils in life and fewer shipwrecks in the world!

If there was a remora on land it was the tongue of Saint Anthony, where, as with the remora, the verse of Saint Gregory Nazianzen shows: *Lingua quidem parva est, sed viribus omnia vincit.*[8] The apostle Saint James in his most eloquent Epistle compares the tongue to the rudder of a ship and the bridle of a horse. Both comparisons put together marvelously describe the qualities of the remora, which, clinging to the rudder of a ship, is the ship's bridle, the rudder of the rudder. And such was the quality and strength of Saint Anthony's tongue. The rudder of human nature is free will, the pilot is reason, but how few times do the hasty drives of the will obey reason?

Concerning this rudder, however, so disobedient and rebellious, Anthony's tongue showed how much strength it had, like the remora, to tame the fury of human passions. How many people chasing fortune on the vessel Pride, its sails inflated with the wind and with pride itself (for it, too, is a wind), would have broken up on the shoals that were already pounding on the prow, if the remora of Anthony's tongue had not put a hand to the rudder until the sails were furled as reason demanded and the storm, outside and inside, ceased? How many people on board the vessel Vengeance, with its artillery at the ready and its torches lighted, running with swollen sails to give battle, would have been burned or gone to the bottom if the remora of Anthony's tongue had not restrained their fury until, their wrath and hatred subdued, they avoided it amicably under a flag of peace? How many people sailing on the vessel Avarice, overloaded to the gunwales and open at all its seams by the weight, unable to flee or defend itself, would have fallen into the hands of pirates with the loss of everything they were carrying and were going in search of if Anthony's tongue, like a remora, had not made them stop until, relieved of that unjust cargo, they got out of danger and made port? How many people on the vessel Sensuality, which always sails in a fog without sun in the daytime or stars at night, enticed by the song of sirens, letting itself be carried along by the current, would have gone on to be lost blindly in Scylla or Charybdis, from where no ship or shipmate ever reappears, if the remora of Anthony's tongue had not held them back until the light made things clear and visible?

That is the tongue, oh, fish, of your great preacher, who was also your remora while you listened to him; and because it is mute now (although still preserved intact), so many shipwrecks are seen and lamented on land.

But let us pass on from the admiration of such a great virtue of yours to the praise or envy of another no lesser one, equally admirable in quality, that belongs to that other small fish the Romans called torpedo. Both of these fish are known to us more by fame than by sight, but this makes their great virtues all the greater the more they are hidden. The fisherman has his rod in hand, the hook is at the bottom, and the float is on the surface, and as the torpedo nibbles at the bait the fisherman's arm begins to tremble. Can there be any quicker and more admirable effect? So in a flash the virtue of that little fish passes from its mouth to the hook, from the hook to the line, from the line to the rod, and from the rod to the fisherman's arm.

I was quite right in saying that this praise of you must be mentioned with envy. Would that the fishermen in our element had been given or received that trembling quality in everything they fish for on land! They fish a lot, but I am not surprised by this quantity; what surprises me is that they fish so much and tremble so little. So much fishing and so little trembling!

We could set up a problem and ask where there are more fishermen and more ways and equipment for fishing, on land or on the sea? It would certainly be on land. I do not wish to run through them, even though it would be a great consolation for the fish. Suffice it for me to make a comparison with the rod, because it is the instrument in our case. At sea they fish with rods, on land with poles (and so many kinds of poles); they fish with batons, they fish with crosiers, they fish with maces, and they even fish with scepters, and they fish more than anything with these last, because they are fishing for cities and whole kingdoms. And how is it possible that when men fish with such heavy things, their hands and arms do not tremble? If I were preaching and had the tongue of Saint Anthony, I would make them tremble.

Twenty-two of these fishermen found themselves listening by chance to a sermon of Saint Anthony's and the saint's words made them all tremble so that all of them, trembling, flung themselves at his feet. All of them, trembling, confessed their thefts. All of them, trembling, gave back what they could (which is what makes a person with that sin tremble more than others). All of them, in the end, changed their lives and occupations and reformed.

I should like to end this discourse on the praises and virtues of fish with one who may or may not have listened to Saint Anthony and learned to preach from him. The fact is that it preached to me and if I had been someone else I, too, would have been converted. Sailing from here to Pará (for it is a good thing not to leave out the fish of our coast), from time to time I would see running along the surface of the water in leaps a school of small fish that I was unfamiliar with. And, as they told me that the Portuguese call them "four-eyes," I tried to ascertain visually the reason for that name and I found that they really do have four eyes, normal and perfect in all respects. Give thanks to God, I told the fish, and praise the liberality of his divine providence toward you, because to eagles, who are the lynxes of the air, he gave only two eyes, and to lynxes, who are the eagles of the land, also two; but to you, little fish, four.

I was even more surprised as I considered the circumstances of that marvel. So many instruments of sight on a little sea creature alongside the shores of those same vast territories where God has permitted so many thousands of people to live in blindness for so many centuries! Oh, how lofty and incomprehensible are the motives of God, and how profound the depths of his judgments!

Philosophizing, then, about the natural cause of that dispensation, I noticed that those four eyes were located somewhat outside the usual place and that each pair of them was joined, like the two glass chambers of an hourglass, so that those on the top side could look directly up and those on the bottom side directly down. And the reason for that new design is that these little fish, who always swim along the surface of the water, are chased not only by other larger fish in the sea, but also by a large number of sea birds who live on those beaches; and since they have enemies at sea and enemies in the air, nature has doubled their sentries and given them two eyes that look directly up to keep watch for birds, and another two that look directly down to keep watch for the fish.

How neatly a rational soul has shaped those four eyes and how neatly they are used, better than in many men! That is the preaching that little fish did for me, teaching me that if I have faith and the use of reason, I should only look straight up and only straight down: up, thinking that there is a Heaven, and down, remembering that there is a Hell. It did not quote me a passage of Scripture for that, but it did teach me what David meant in one that I had not understood: *Averte oculos meos, ne videant vanitatem.* "Turn away my eyes from looking at worthless things."[10]

Well, could not David have turned his eyes to where he wanted? Not in the way he wanted. He wanted his eyes turned in such a way that they would not see vanity, and that he could not do in this world, no matter where he turned his eyes, because in this world "all is vanity": *Vanitas vanitatum et omnia vanitas.*[11] Therefore, in order for David's eyes not to see vanity, God would have to turn them so they would only see and look toward the other World in both its hemispheres; or, upward, looking directly only at Heaven, or, downward, looking directly only at Hell. And that is the grace which that great prophet asked of God, and this is the doctrine preached to me by that so tiny little fish.

Even though Heaven and Hell were not made for you, brethren fish, I shall end and complete your praises by giving you thanks for the great help you have given for their going to Heaven and not to Hell to those who are nourished by you. You are the nourishment of Carthusians and Carmelites and all the holy families that profess the most rigorous austerity. You are the ones who help all true Christians endure the penitence of Lent. You are the ones on whom Christ himself feasted at Eastertide the two times he ate with his disciples after his resurrection. Let birds and land animals boast of making splendid and costly banquets for the rich, while you glory in being the companions of the fasting and abstinence of the just! All of you have so much kinship and affinity with virtue that while God has forbidden even the vilest and most vulgar meat from days of fasting, he has allowed the finest and most delicate flesh of fish. And although only two days of the week are called yours, no day is forbidden you. Astrologers only gave you one place among the celestial signs, but those on earth who sustain themselves only on you are the ones most assured of finding a place in Heaven. Lastly, you are the creatures of that element whose fruitfulness above all belongs to the Holy Spirit: *Spiritus Domini faecundabat aquas.*[12]

God laid down his blessing upon you to grow and multiply, and so the Lord may confirm his blessing on you, remember not to forsake the poor with your care. Be aware that in the sustenance of the poor you sustain your growth. Take the example of your sisters the sardines. Why do you think the Creator has multiplied them in such uncountable numbers? Because they are the sustenance of the poor. Sturgeon and salmon are very few in number because they are served at the tables of kings and the powerful, but the fish that nourishes Christ's poor is multiplied and increased by Christ himself. The two fishes that accompanied the five loaves in the desert were multiplied so much that they fed five thousand men. So if dead fish that nourish the poor can multiply that much, how much greater and better can the living do so! Grow, fish, grow and multiply, and may God confirm his blessing on you.

IV

Before you go, however, just as you have heard your praises, listen now to your reprimands as well. They will only serve to confuse you since you cannot make amends. The first thing that distresses me about you, fish, is that you eat each other. This is a great scandal, but the circumstances make it even greater. Not only do you eat each other, but the large eat the small. If it were the other way around it would not be so bad. If the small ones ate the large, one large one would be sufficient for many small ones; but since the large eat the small, not even a hundred, not even a thousand are enough for one large one. Note how Saint Augustine was surprised at this: *Homines pravis, praeversisque cupiditatibus facti sunt, sicut pisces invicem se devorantes.* "Men with their greater and perverse greed, are becoming like fish, who eat each other." How alien it is, not only to reason, but to nature itself, that all of you being creatures in the same element, all of you citizens of the same nation, and all of you brethren in the end, live by eating each other! Saint Augustine, who was preaching to men, in order to heighten the ugliness of this scandal illustrated it for them by means of fish, and I, who preach to fish, in order for you to see how ugly and abominable it is, want you to see it in men.

Take a look, you fish in the sea there, at the land. No, no, that's not where I mean. Are you turning your eyes to the forests and wastelands? Look this way, this way, look at the town here. Do you think that only Tapuia Indians eat each other? There is a much larger slaughterhouse here and white men eat each other much more. Do you see all that bustle, all that movement, see that gathering on the squares and that crossing of streets, see that walking up and down the sidewalks, that going in and out without cease or rest? Well, all of that is men going about seeking to eat and be eaten. When one of them dies, you will quickly see how many there are assembling over the unfortunate person, tearing him apart and eating him. His heirs eat him, his executors eat him, his legatees eat him, his creditors eat him, the surrogates of orphans eat him, those of the dead and absent eat him, the doctor who took care of him or helped him die eats him, the bleeder who took out his blood eats him, even his wife eats him when, grudgingly, she gives him the oldest sheet in the house for a shroud, the one who digs his grave eats him, the one who rings the bells and those who bear him to his burial singing eat him; in short, even before the poor decedent has eaten the dust of the earth the entire earth has eaten him up.

Still, if men were to eat each other only after death, it seems that would not be so horrible or exercise feelings so much. But so you can see how far your cruelty reaches, consider, fish, that men also eat each other alive, the same as you. Job was alive when he said: *Quare persequimini me, et carnibus meis saturamini?* "Why do you persecute me so inhumanly, you who are eating me alive and glutting yourselves with my flesh?"[13] Would you like to see one of those Jobs?

Take a look at one of those men persecuted by lawsuits or accused of a crime and see how many people are eating him. The bailiff is eating him, the jailer is eating him, the scribe is eating him, the solicitor is eating him, the barrister is eating him, the investigator is eating him, the witness is eating him, the judge is eating him, and although he still has not been sentenced, he has already been eaten. Men are worse than crows. The poor fellow who goes to the gallows is not eaten by the crows until after he has been executed and is dead, but the one who is still on trial has neither been sentenced nor executed yet and is already eaten.

And so you will see how those eaten on land are the little ones and in the same way that you eat each other in the sea, listen to God as he complains of that sin: *Nonne cognoscent omnes, qui perantur iniquitatem, qui devorant plebem meam, ut cibum panis?*[14] "Do you think that the time shall not come," God says, "when those who work evil understand what they have done and pay what they deserve?" And what evil is the one that God singles out to call evil, as if there were no other on earth? And who are those who commit it? The evil is the eating of men by others, and the ones who commit it are the larger who eat the smaller. *Qui devorant plebem meam, ut cibum panis.*

What is of concern and consequence in those words, fish, where you can notice so many other things, are the words themselves. God says that men not only eat his people, but, declaredly, his plebes: *Plebem meam*, because the plebes and the plebeians, who are the smallest, the ones who can do the least and who count the least in the republic, these are the ones being eaten. And he not only says that they are merely eaten, but that they are swallowed and devoured: *Qui devorant*. Because the great ones who rule cities and provinces do not sate their hunger by eating the small one by one, or a few at a time, but they devour and swallow entire peoples: *Qui devorant plebem meam*. And how do they devour and eat them? *Ut cibum panis*: not like other foods, but like bread.

The difference between bread and other foods is that there are meat days for meat and fish days for fish, and different months of the year for fruit. Bread, however, is food for every day, always, continuously eaten, and that is how little people suffer. They are the daily bread of the great. And just as bread is eaten with everything, so too are the miserable little people eaten with everything and in everything, with no recourse against being carried off, fined, swindled, eaten, swallowed, devoured: *Qui devorant plebem meam, ut cibum panis.*

Do you think that is right, fish? I can see by the way you are shaking your heads that you are all saying no, and by the way you are looking at each other you are surprised and astonished that such injustice and wickedness could exist among men. Well, it is just the same as you do. The large eat the small, and the very large not only eat them one by one, but by whole schools, and continuously, with no difference by season, not only by day, but also by night, in the light and in the dark, as men also do.

If you think, however, that these injustices among you are tolerated and go without punishment, you are mistaken. Just as God punishes them in men, so, too, in his way does he punish them in you. The oldest who are listening to me and are present here have surely seen it in this State and have heard, at least, passengers in canoes muttering, and their poor rowers lamenting even more, that the great ones who were sent here, instead of governing and helping this State prosper, have destroyed it, because they have satisfied all the hunger they brought with them by eating and devouring the small.

That is how it was, but if there might be some among you who followed the course of the ships, went with them to Portugal and returned to the seas of the mother country, you might well have heard back there in the Tagus that those same larger ones who ate the small ones here, when they arrive there find others larger who also eat them. This is the style of divine justice so ancient and manifest that even the pagans knew it and celebrated it:

> Vos quibus rector maris, atque terrae
> Jus dedit magnum necis, atque vitae;
> Ponite inflatos, tumidosque vultus;
> Quidquid a vobis minor extimescit,
> Maior hoc vobis dominus minatur.[15]

Take note, fish, of that defnition of God: *Rector maris atque terrae*, "Governor of sea and land," so that you will have no doubt that the same style God uses with men on land he also observes with you in the sea. It is necessary, then, for you to look to yourselves and pay close attention to the doctrine given you by the great Doctor of the Church, Saint Ambrose, who, when speaking to you, said: *Cave nedum alium insequeris, incidas in validorem*, "Let the fish who pursues the weaker to eat beware that he does not find himself in the mouth of one stronger" who will gobble him up. We see it here every day. The jackfish goes chasing after the catfish, just as the hound goes after the hare, and is blind to the shark with four rows of teeth behind him who will swallow him in one mouthful. That is what Saint Augustine told you with more elegance: *Praedo minoris fit praeda maioris*.[16] But these examples are not enough, fish, to persuade your greed finally that the same cruelty you use with the small is always matched by the punishment of the voracity of the large.

Since that is how you experience it with so much damage to yourselves, it is important that from here on you be better citizens and more zealous of the commonweal, and that this prevail over the particular appetite of each one so that it will not occur, as we see today, that so many of you, already diminished, are completely consumed. Is it not enough that there

be so many outside enemies and pursuers as wily and persistent as fishermen who desist neither by day nor by night in besieging you and making
war in so many ways? Can you not see them weaving and entangling their
nets to use against you, setting their traps against you, casting their lines
against you, bending and sharpening their hooks against you, grasping
their spears and harpoons against you? Can you not see that even reeds are
lances and corks offensive weapons against you? Is it not enough, then, for
you to have so many and such well-armed enemies outside without your
being crueler inside too, chasing each other in a more than civil war and
eating each other up? Cease, cease, at last, brethren fish, and put an end
one day to such pernicious discord; and since I have called you brethren
and you are brothers, remember the obligations of that name. Were you
not quite calm, quite peaceful, and good friends all, large and small, when
Saint Anthony preached to you? Well, continue that way and you will be
happy.

You will probably tell me (as men also do) that you have no other way
to nourish yourselves. So what do the many among you who do not eat the
others nourish themselves upon? The sea is very vast, very fertile, very abundant, and a large part of those who live within it can sustain themselves on
what it casts up on the shore alone. The feeding of some animals upon others is voracity and abuse and not a law of nature. Those on land and in the
air who eat each other today did not eat each other at the beginning of the
world because it was proper and necessary for the species to multiply then.
The same thing (even more clearly) obtained after the flood, because as only
two of each species had escaped they could scarcely have preserved themselves if they ate each other. And, finally, during the time of the same flood
in which all lived together inside the ark, the wolf watched the lamb, the
hawk the quail, the lion the deer, and every one of those they were accustomed to feed upon; and if there was any temptation there they all resisted
it and adjusted to the rations of the common stores that Noah divided
among them. So if the animals of the other warmer elements were capable
of that temperance, why should not those of the water be? In short, if on so
many occasions through the natural desire for their own preservation and
increase they made a virtue of necessity, you should do so too, or make it a
virtue without necessity and it will be an even greater virtue.

Another quite common thing in many of you that wounds me even
more than it disheartens me is the ever so notable blindness and ignorance
that those who navigate in these parts feel. When a man of the sea takes a
hook, ties a piece of cloth cut so that it opens up into two or three points

onto it, throws it out on a thin line until it touches the water, and when a fish sees it and attacks it blindly and gets caught, gasping until, hanging like that in the air or tossed up onto the deck, he finally dies, can there be any greater ignorance and arrant blindness than that? Tricked into losing their lives over a snippet of cloth?

You will probably tell me that men do the same thing. I am not going to deny it. An army gives battle to another army, men are caught by the tips of pikes, spears, and swords, and why? Because there was someone who enticed them with two pieces of cloth. Among the vices vanity is the most astute fisherman and the one that most easily tricks men. And what does vanity do? It places as a banner on the tip of those pikes, those spears, and those swords two pieces of cloth, either white, which is called the habit of Malta, or green, which is called the habit of Avis, or red, which is called the habit of Christ and Saint James; and the men, as they come to pass that piece of cloth through their breast, do not notice what they are swallowing and they swallow the iron. And then what happens? The same as with you. The one who swallowed the iron, either then or on another occasion, was killed; and the same pieces of cloth go back to the hook again to fish for others.

With that example I concede, fish, that men do the same as you, although I do not think this was a basis for your answer or excuse because here in the Maranhão, even though a lot of blood is spilled, there are no armies or the ambitions of those habits.

But not for that reason either will I deny to you that here, too, men let themselves be fished by the same deception in a more ignorant and less honorable fashion. Who is fishing for the lives of all the men in the Maranhão and with what? A man of the sea with a few strips of cloth. A ship's master comes from Portugal with four sweepings from shops, four pieces of cloth, and four pieces of silk whose time has passed and which have not been worn out yet, and what does he do? He baits the inhabitants of our land with those rags: he gives them a tug and gives them another so that each time the price goes up, and the pretty ones, or the ones who want to be pretty, all starving for the rags, remain there gagging and caught with debts from one year to the next, and from one crop to the next, and there goes life. This is not an exaggeration. All of them work all their lives on farms, in canefields, in mills, in tobacco fields, and what does this lifetime of work bring them? It does not bring them coaches or litters or horses or squires or pages or lackeys or tapestries or paintings or tableware or jewels; so what does their whole life depend on? On the sad rags they wear out into the street, and for this they kill themselves the whole year.

Is this not, my dear fish, a great madness in men that you are exempt from? Of course it is, and you cannot deny it. So if it is great madness to waste one's life for a couple of cuts of cloth on the part of those who have an obligation to dress up, for you, whom God has dressed from head to toe either with skins of showy and appropriate colors or silver and golden scales that never tear or wear out with time or vary or ever change with fashion, is it not greater ignorance and greater blindness to let yourselves be tricked or let yourselves be caught by the lips with two strips of cloth? Look at your Saint Anthony, whom the world was unable to trick with those vanities. Being a noble young man, he abandoned the display which that age prized so much, exchanged it for a cassock of serge and the sash of a monk, and after he saw that a costume like that was still an expensive shroud, he exchanged serge for coarse wool and the sash for a rope. With that rope and that cloth he fished for many and they were the only ones who were not deceived and were prudent.

V

Getting down to cases, I shall say now, fish, what I have against some of you, and beginning here on our coast. On the same day that I arrived, hearing the fish called grunts, or braggarts for some, and seeing their size, I was moved to both laughter and to anger. Is it possible that being such tiny little fish you are the braggarts of the sea? If a cripple can catch you with a piece of sewing thread and a bent pin, why should you grunt and brag so much? But that is the very reason for your bragging. Tell me, why does not the swordfish grunt or brag? Because someone with a good sword ordinarily does not have much of a tongue. That is not a general rule, but it is a general rule that God does not like braggarts and he takes particular care to bring down and humiliate those who do a lot of boasting. Saint Peter, whom your ancestors knew quite well, had such a good sword that he alone went up against a whole army of Roman soldiers and if Christ had not ordered him to sheathe it, I can assure that he would have cut off more ears than just that of Malchus. Yet, what happened that same night? Peter had boasted and bragged that if all of them weakened, only he would be constant unto death if necessary, and it all turned out so much the opposite that only he weakened more than all the others, and the voice of a little woman was enough to make him tremble and deny. Before that he had already weakened at the very time he promised so much for himself. Christ told him in the garden to keep watch and when he came there shortly after to see if he was doing so, he found him asleep, with such a lack of care that he not only awakened him out of his sleep, but also out of what he had boasted: *Sic non potuisti una hora vigilare mecum?*[17] You, Peter, are the brave one who was to die for me, "and could you not watch one hour?" So much bragging a little while back and so much sleeping now? But that was what happened. A lot of bragging before the occasion is the sign of sleeping through it. So what do you think of that, brother grunts, called braggarts? If that happened to the greatest of fishermen, what can happen to the least of fish? Take measure of yourselves and you will see what little basis there is for your boasting and grunting.

If whales boasted their arrogance they would have more excuse because of their great size. But not even whales could maintain that arrogance. What the whale is among fish, the giant Goliath was among men. If the River Jordan and the Sea of Galilee have communication with the Ocean, as they must, for everything flows from them, you surely must know that that giant was the bragging grunt of the Philistines. For forty days he stood armed in the field challenging the whole encampment of Israel with no one daring to come forward. And in the end what was the outcome of such arrogance? It took a mere shepherd boy with a sling and a crook to bring him down. The arrogant and prideful challenge God, and whoever challenges God always comes crashing down. So, friend grunts, my true advice is for you to be silent and imitate Saint Anthony. There are two things men have that usually make the grunting braggarts because both things puff them up: knowledge and power. Caiaphas bragged of knowledge: *Vos nescitis quidquam.*[18] Pilate bragged of power: *Nescis quia potestam habeo?*[19] And both against Christ. But Christ's faithful servant Anthony, having so much knowledge, as I have already told you, and so much power, as you yourselves have experienced, had no one who had ever heard him speak of knowledge and power, much less boast about it. And his being so silent was precisely why he gave such a roar.

On the trip I mentioned and on all the ones on which I crossed the Equator, I looked below and saw what many times I had seen and noted in men, and I was surprised that the disease had spread out and got to fish too. The ones I am talking about now are called shark suckers or clingers because, being small, they not only come up to other larger fish, but cling to their sides in such a way that they never let go. They say that some animals of less strength will follow hunting lions from a distance to live off what they leave behind. These clingers do the same, precisely the same from close by as the others do from a distance, because the big fish cannot turn its head or its mouth around onto the ones it carries on its back, and so it bears their weight and their hunger as well.

This way of life, more wily than generous, may have passed from one element to the other and taken hold there, with the fish learning it on the high seas after our Portuguese had sailed them, because no viceroy or governor ever leaves for the conquered lands without going off surrounded by clingers who live off him, so that he satisfies here the hunger they had no way of satisfying there. The less ignorant, schooled by experience, break away and earn their livelihood by other means, but those who let themselves cling to the favor and fortune of the greater find themselves victims of the same end as the clingers of the sea.

The shark circles the ship in the equatorial doldrums with his clingers on his back, so stitched to the skin that they look more like patches or natural spots than guests or traveling companions. A hook on a chain baited with the rations of four soldiers is tossed to him and he furiously attacks the prey, swallows it in one gulp, and is caught. Half of the ship's company runs and hauls him aboard as he thrashes wildly against the deck in his last struggles. Finally the shark dies and with him die the clingers.

I seem to be hearing Saint Matthew, who was not the fisherman apostle, describing this very thing on land. With the death of Herod, the Evangelist says, the angel appeared to Joseph in Egypt and told him that he could now return to his homeland because "those who sought the young Child's life are dead": *Defuncti sunt enim qui quaerebant animam Pueri.*[20] Those who wished to take the life of the Christ Child were Herod and all his people, all his family, all his followers, all those who followed and depended on his fortune. Well, is it possible that all of them died along with Herod? Yes, because with the death of the shark the clingers also die: *Defuncto Herode, defuncti sunt qui quaerebant animam Pueri.*[21]

Behold here, ignorant and miserable little fish, how mistaken and deceptive this way of life you have chosen is. Take your example from men, as they will not take theirs from you or follow that of Saint Anthony as they should.

God also has his clingers. One of these was David, who said: *Mihi autem adhaerere Deo bonum est.*[22] Let them cling to the great of the earth, for "I only wish to cling to God." That is what Saint Anthony does too; and just behold the Saint himself and see how he clings to Christ and Christ to him. One can truly wonder which of the two is the clinger there, and it would appear to be Christ, because the smaller is always the one who clings to the larger, and the Lord has made himself tiny so he can cling to Anthony. But Anthony has also made himself smaller so that he can cling more to God. It follows from this that all who cling to God, who is immortal, are safe

from dying like the other clingers. And so safe that even in the case where
God became man and died, he only died so that all of those who clung to
him would not die: *Si ergo me quaeritis, sinite hos abire*, "Therefore, if you
seek me, let these go their way."[23] And although only men can cling in this
way, and you, my little fish, cannot, you must at least imitate the other
animals of the air and land who, when they get close to the large ones and
seek the shelter of their power, do not cling in such a way that they will die
along with them. Scripture speaks of that famous tree that stood for the great
Nebuchadnezzar, where all the birds of the sky rested on its branches and all
the animals of the land gathered under its shade, and both kinds sustained
themselves on its fruit, but it also tells how, as soon as that tree was cut, the
birds flew away and all the animals ran off. Draw close to the great, then, but
do not cling so closely that you will be killed by them or die with them.

Consider, living clingers, how those others who clung to that large fish
died and why. The shark died because he ate and they died from what they
did not eat. Can there be any greater ignorance than dying because of the
hunger of someone else's mouth? Let the shark die because he ate, his greed
killed him; but for the clinger to die for what he did not eat is the greatest
misfortune imaginable. Do not think that in fish, too, original sin existed.
We men were so unfortunate that somebody else ate and we are paying for it.
Our deaths have their beginning in the gluttony of Adam and Eve, and the
fact that we must die for what someone else ate is a great misfortune! But we
can wash ourselves clean of that misfortune with a little water, and you cannot wash yourselves clean of your ignorance with all the water in the sea.

I also have some words for flying fish, and the complaint is not a small
one. Tell me, flying fish, did not God make you to be fish? So what possessed
you to be birds? God made the sea for you and the air for them. Content
yourselves with the sea and with swimming, and do not try to fly, because
you are fish. If you do not know yourselves, perhaps, look at your fins and
your scales and you will find out that you are not birds, but fish, and even
among fish not the best. You will probably tell me, flying fish, that God gave
you bigger fins than others your size. So just because you had larger fins, was
that any reason to make wings of them? But it is even worse because your
punishment deceives you so many times. You wanted to be better than other
fish and therefore you are more wretched than all of them. The other fish
in the sea are killed by hook or gaff; you, without hook or gaff, are killed by
your own arrogance and pride. A ship comes sailing along with the sailor
asleep and a flying fish hits a sail or a rope and falls thrashing. Other fish are
killed by hunger and the bait tricks them, the flying fish is killed by its vanity

in flying and its bait is the wind. How much better it would be for it to dive beneath the keel and live than fly over the rigging and fall down dead!

It is a great ambition, with the sea being so immense, for all the sea not to be enough for a small fish as it wants an even broader element. But see, fish, the punishment for ambition. God made the flying fish a fish and it wanted to be a bird, and God himself allows it to have the dangers of a bird along with those of a fish. All the sails are nets for it as a fish and all the rigging is a snare for it as a bird. See, flying fish, what punishment lies in wait for you. A while back you were swimming alive in the sea with your fins and now you lie on a deck with your wings as your shrouds. Not content with being a fish, you wanted to be a bird, and now you are neither bird nor fish, you can no longer either fly or swim. Nature gave you the water, you only wanted the air, and I can already see you roasting over the fire. Fish, be content, each of you, with your element. If the flying fish had not wanted to go from the second to the third, it would not have ended up in the fourth. It was quite safe from fire while swimming in the water, but because it wanted to be a moth of the waves it got its wings singed.

In view of this example, fish, memorize this saying: He who wants more than he's got loses what he has and what he's not. For one who can swim and wants to fly the time will come when he neither flies nor swims. Listen to the case of a flier on land: Simon Magus, whose surname came from the magic art for which he was most famous, pretending that he was the true son of God predicted the day when before the eyes of all Rome he would rise up to Heaven, and he did in fact begin to fly quite high. The prayers of Saint Peter, who was present, flew faster than he, however, and when the magician fell from on high, God did not want him to die right away, but for him to be broken in the eyes of all, so he fractured his legs.

I am not asking you to look at the punishment but at its type. It was a good thing that Simon fell; if he had died right away, it would have been a good thing too, as his insolence and diabolical art deserved. But why was it that from a fall that high he did not shatter or break his skull and arms, only his feet? Yes, says Saint Maximus, because one who has feet to walk with and wants wings to fly with should properly lose both wings and feet. The Holy Father says elegantly: *Ut qui paulo ante volare tentaverat, subito ambulare non posset; et qui pennas assumpserat, plantas amitteret.*[24] If Simon has feet and wants wings, can walk and wants to fly, then let his wings be broken so that he will not fly and also his feet so he cannot walk. Behold, fliers of the sea, what happens to those on land, so that each one of you will be content in his element. If the sea had followed the example of rivers after Icarus drowned in the Danube, there would not be so many Icaruses in the Ocean.

Oh, soul of Anthony, only you had wings and flew without danger because you learned to fly low and not up! Saint John had already seen in his Revelation that woman whose adornments absorbed all the light of the Firmament and he says that she "was given two wings of a great eagle": *Datae sunt mulieri alae duae aquilae magnae.* And for what? *Ut volaret in desertum,* "to fly into the wilderness."[25] A noteworthy thing that the prophet himself did not call a great miracle in vain. That woman was in Heaven: *Signum magnum apparauit in coelo, mulier amicta sole.*[26] So if the woman was in Heaven and the desert was on earth, why was she given wings to fly into the wilderness? Because there are wings for ascending and wings for descending. The wings for ascending are very dangerous, the wings for descending very safe, and such were Saint Anthony's. Saint Anthony's soul was given two eagle wings, which were that sublime double wisdom, natural and supernatural, as we know. And what did he do? He did not spread his wings to ascend, he folded them to descend, and so tightly that he, the Ark of the Testament, was reputed, as I have already told you, to be an artless person without knowledge. Fliers of the sea (I am not speaking to those on land), imitate your preaching saint. If you think that your fins can serve as wings, do not spread them for ascending, because you will only succeed in running into some sail or a ship's broadside. Fold them to descend, go plunge into the depths of some cave. The more hidden you are there, the safer you will be.

But since we are in the caves of the sea now, before we come out of them we have brother octopus there, against whom no less than Saints Basil and Ambrose have their complaints. The octopus, with that hood of his over his head, looks like a monk. With those rays of his extended arms he looks like a star. With that lack of bones or spine he looks like softness and gentleness itself. And underneath that modest appearance, or that so saintly hypocrisy, the two great Doctors of the Greek and Latin Churches bear constant witness to the fact that the octopus is the most treacherous creature of the sea. The treachery of the octopus consists first in dressing himself or painting himself in the same colors as all the colors he is clinging to. The colors that in the chameleon are decoration, in the octopus are cunning. The shapes that in Proteus are a fable, in the octopus are the truth and a trick. If he is on moss, he makes himself green. If he is on sand, he makes himself white. If he is on mud, he makes himself gray. And if he is on some stone, as he usually is, he makes himself the color of that stone. So what is the result of all this? What happens is that another fish, unaware of the treachery, passes by unconcerned and the bandit, who is in ambush inside his own deceit, throws out his arms and makes it prisoner. Did Judas do any more than that? He did not do more because he did not do as much. Judas embraced Christ, but others took him. The octopus is the one who embraces and also the one who takes. Judas gave the signal with his arms, but the octopus makes ropes of his arms. Judas, it is true, was treacherous, but with lanterns before him: he had planned his treachery in the dark, but he carried it out in full light. The octopus, darkening himself, takes the sight of others away, and the first step of treachery and theft he takes is against the light so that colors cannot be made out. See, perfidious and vile fish, the measure of your evil, for Judas, as compared to you, is less treacherous!

Oh, such an excess of effrontery and indignity for such a pure, clear, and crystalline element as water, the natural mirror not only of the land but of the very sky! As the prophet says in appreciation of that, "even waters are dark in the clouds of the air": *Tenebrosa aqua in nubibus aeris.*[27] And he was speaking precisely of the clouds in the air in order to attribute darkness to the other element and not to water, which, in its own element, is always clear, diaphanous and transparent, where nothing can hide, cover, or disguise itself. And to think that in that same element there breeds, survives, and works with such harm for the public good a monster so deceitful, so false, so astute, so tricky, and so skillfully treacherous!

I see, fish, that from the knowledge you have of the lands on which your seas break, you are answering me and agreeing that there, too, there is falseness, deception, pretense, fraud, ambushes, and even greater and more pernicious treachery. And on the same subject that you defend, you could also apply another property to your fellows that is very much their own, but since you do not mention it, I, too, shall remain quiet. With great confusion, however, I confess everything and much more than you say, because I cannot deny it. But cast your eyes on Anthony, your preacher, and you will see in him the purest example of candor, sincerity, and truth, where there never was any deceit, pretense, or trickery. And know, too, that in order for each of us to have all of that it once was enough to be Portuguese, one did not have to be a saint.

I have finished your praises and rebukes, brethren fish, and I have satisfied, as I promised you, the two obligations of salt, although the one from the sea and not the one of the earth: *Vos estis sal terrae.* All that remains is to give a necessary warning to you who live in these seas. Since they are so broken up and full of shoals, you know quite well that many ships founder and are lost, by which the sea is enriched and the land impoverished. You must take heed, then, that with this very wealth you run a great risk, because all those who take advantage of the goods of shipwrecks are excommunicated and cursed.

This pain of excommunication, which is most serious, is not placed on you but on men, although God has shown clearly many times that when animals commit materially what is forbidden by this law they too incur the pains of it in their own way and at the same point begin to waste away until they come to a miserable end.

Christ ordered Saint Peter to go fishing and said that in the mouth of the first fish he caught he would find a coin with which to pay a certain tribute. If Peter was to catch more fish than that one, assuming that it was the first taken, with the price of it and the others he would have been able to make enough money to pay that tribute, which was only that of a silver coin of no great weight. With what mystery, then, does the Lord order him to take it out of the mouth of that fish and that it should be the one to die before the others?

Pay attention now. Fish do not mint coins at the bottom of the sea, nor do they have contracts with men from which money might be forthcoming. Therefore the coin that this fish had swallowed was from some ship that had foundered in those seas. And the Lord wished to show that the punishment that Saint Peter and his successors called down upon those who take the wealth of shipwreck victims also obtains with fish who incur it in their own way by being the first to die and because of the very coin that they swallowed sticking in their throats.

Oh, what a fine doctrine this would be for the land, if I had not preached it to the sea! For men there is no more miserable death than to die with someone else's property stuck in their throat, because it is a sin that not even Saint Peter, not even the Supreme Pontiff can absolve. And although men incur eternal death, which fish are not capable of, fish can still hasten their temporal one, as in this case, when, as I have said, they do not leave the property of shipwreck victims materially alone.

VI

I dismiss you with this last piece of advice, or I take leave of you with it, my fish. And so that you may go away consoled by the sermon, because I do not know when you will hear another, I want to relieve you of a very ancient and disconsoling matter that has been with all of you ever since the writing of Leviticus. In the ecclesiastical or ritualistic law in Leviticus, God chose certain animals that were to be sacrificed to him, but all of them either land animals or birds, with fish being totally excluded from the sacrifices. And who can doubt that such a universal exclusion of this was worthy of great disconsolation and feeling on the part of all the inhabitants of an element so noble that it was worthy of providing the material for the first sacrament? The main reason for excluding fish was because the other animals would go alive to the sacrifice and fish generally not, but, rather, dead, and God does not want any dead thing to be offered to him or to reach his altars. This point would also be very important and necessary for men if I were preaching to them. Oh, how many souls come to that altar dead because they come and have no horror of coming while in mortal sin! Fish, give great thanks to God for having freed you from that danger, because it is better not to come to the sacrifice than to come dead. Let other animals offer themselves to God to be sacrificed, you offer yourselves by not coming to the sacrifice. Let the others sacrifice their lives and blood to God, you sacrifice for him in your respect and reverence.

Oh, fish, how I envy you that natural irregularity! How much better it would be for me not to take God in my hands than to take him unworthily! With all that I outstrip you in, fish, I recognize many advantages on your side. Your brutish state is better than my reason and your instinct better than my free will. I can speak, but you do not offend God with words. I remember things, but you do not offend God with memory. I think things through, but you do not offend God with understanding. I want, but you do not offend God with wishes. You were created by God to serve mankind and you attained the end for which you were created. I was created to serve him and I have not attained the end for which he created me. You were not to see God and yet you will be able to appear before him very confidently because you have not offended him. I hope that I am to see him, but with what face am I to appear before his divine scrutiny if I do not cease offending him? Oh, I am close to saying that it would have been better for me to have been like you, for of a man who had the same obligations the Supreme Truth said that "it would have been better for him not to have been born a man": *Si natus non fuisset homo ille.*[28] And since we who were born men respond so poorly to the obligations of our birth, be happy, fish, and give great thanks to God for yours.

Benedicite, cete et omnis quae moventur in aquis, Domino: "Praise God, fish, the large and the small," and, divided into two choruses of countless numbers, praise all of you in unison. Praise God because he has created so many of you. Praise God who has distinguished you with so many species; praise God who has dressed you with such variety and beauty; praise God who has equipped you with all the instruments necessary for life; praise God who has given you such a vast and pure element; praise God who, coming into this world, lived among you and called to him those who lived with you and off you; praise God who sustains you; praise God who preserves you; praise God who increases you; praise God, finally, by serving and sustaining mankind, which is the end he created for you; and just as he gave you his blessing in the beginning so will he do so now also. Amen. Since you are not capable of Glory or Grace, your sermon does not end in Grace and Glory.

Maundy Thursday Sermon
Preached in the Royal Chapel in the year 1645

Sciens Jesus quia venit hora ejus, ut
transeat ex hoc mundo ad Patrem, cum dilexisset
suos, qui erant in mundo, in finem dilexit eos.[1]
John 13:1

I

Considering with some care the most singular terms of this loving Gospel
and pondering the harmony and correspondence of its complete discourse
so ingeniously construed so many times, I have come to notice finally (I do
not know whether with as much reason as novelty) that the principal aim
of the Gospel was to demonstrate Christ's knowledge and the principal
aim of Christ was to demonstrate men's ignorance.

Christ knew (Saint John says) that "His hour had come that He should
depart from this world to the Father": *Sciens quia venit hora ejus, ut transeat*
ex hoc mundo ad Patrem. He knew that "the Father had given all things into
His hands, and that He had come from God and was going to God": *Sciens*
quia omnis dedit ei Pater in manus, et quia a Deo exivit, et ad Deum vadit.[2]
He knew that among the twelve who had sat down at his table there was
one who was unfaithful to him and "who would betray him": *Sciebat enim*
quisnam esset qui traderet enim.[3] Up to here the Evangelist has shown Christ's
knowledge. From this point Christ will go on to show the ignorance of men.
When Saint Peter did not wish to let the Lord wash his feet, the Divine Master pointed out his ignorance, saying *Quod ego facio, tu nescis*: "What I am
doing you do not know."[4] When that ever so prodigious example of humility was done, the Lord sat down again and, turning to his Disciples, asked
them, *Scitis quid fecerim vobis?*, "Do you know what I have done to you?"[5]

That emphatic question had the strength of an affirmation, and asking them "do you know?" was saying that they did not know. So in the first part of the Gospel the Evangelist has taken care to demonstrate Christ's knowledge and Christ, in the second, has done so to demonstrate men's ignorance.

But if the aim and intent of both was the same, if the aim and intent of Christ and the Evangelist was to show gloriously to the world the perfection of his love, why does the Evangelist turn completely to pondering Christ's knowledge and Christ to calling attention to men's ignorance? The reason that occurs to me, and I consider it to be true and well founded, is that the two suppositions of Christ's love on this day that are in closest harmony were, on Christ's part, his knowledge and, on men's part, their ignorance. If on Christ's part, as he loved, there could be ignorance, and on men's part, as they were loved, there could be knowledge, even if the Lord had produced the same excesses in us, both they and his love (not in cost but in esteem) would be of greatly inferior worth. Because for the world to lift its thoughts up from vulgar considerations and begin to feel Christ's graces as highly as they deserve, let it be noted (the Evangelist says) that Christ loved knowing, *Sciens Jesus*, and let it be noted (Christ says) that men were loved not knowing: *Tu nescis*.

The thought is suggested, but I can see quite well that it has not been declared. In accordance with and as confirmation of it, I intend to show on this day that only Christ loved truly because he loved knowing: *Sciens*; and only men were loved truly because they were loved not knowing: *Nescis*. But with the *sciens* and the *nescis*, or the *nescis* and the *sciens* mingling and changing places in such a way that with ignorance on the part of men and knowledge on the part of Christ, Christ loved knowing as if he were loving not knowing, and men were loved not knowing as if they were being loved knowing. Let love go along now untangling these threads and I hope that all will see their subtlety.

II

First, only Christ loved because he loved knowing: *Sciens*. For an understanding of this loving truth we must suppose another no less certain truth, and it is that in the world and among men what is commonly called love is not love, it is ignorance. The ancients painted love as a child and the reason, I said last year, was because no love lasts long enough to reach old age. But that interpretation is countered by the example of Jacob and Rachel, that of Jonathan and David, and other great ones, albeit few in number.

So if there is also a love that lasts many years, why do wise men always paint it as a boy? This time I believe I shall find the cause. Love is always painted as a child because even it if lasts beyond seven years, like Jacob's, it never reaches the age of the use of reason. The use of reason and love are two things that are never joined together. What can the soul of a child get to be? A will with affection and an understanding without use. Such is ordinary love. Love conquers all when it conquers a soul, but the first to surrender is understanding. No one has a feverish will without having a frantic understanding. Love will cease varying if it is firm, but it will not cease raving if it is love. Fire has never scorched the will without the smoke blinding understanding. There has never been an illness of the heart that was not weakness in judgment. That is why those same painters of love blindfolded his eyes. And since the first effect or the last disposition of love is to blind the understanding, it follows that what is commonly called love is in the greater part ignorance, and the number of parts it has of ignorance is the same number of lacks it has in love. A person who loves because he knows is a lover, a person who loves because he is ignorant is a fool. Just as ignorance in an offense lessens the crime, in love it lessens the worth. Someone who offends not knowing is really not a delinquent, someone who loves not knowing is not really a lover.

Such is the dependence that love has on these two suppositions that what appears to be goodness, based on ignorance, is not love and what does not appear to be love, based on knowledge, is great goodness. The two most important people in this Gospel will give us the proof: Christ and Saint Peter. Christ was transfigured on Mount Tabor and when Saint Peter saw that the Lord was talking with Moses and Elijah about going to die in Jerusalem, in order to turn him away from death, he advised him to stay there: *Domine, bonum est nos his esse.*[6] This determination of Saint Peter's, taken as Origen took it, was the greatest act of love that has been made or can be made in the world, because if Christ did not go to die in Jerusalem, mankind would not be redeemed; if mankind were not redeemed, Saint Peter would be unable to go to Heaven; and for the great Apostle to wish to deprive himself of the glory of Heaven so that Christ should not die on Earth, for him to place the temporal life of his Lord ahead of his eternal life was the greatest goodness of love that the most valiant of hearts could aspire to. Let us leave Saint Peter and turn to Christ, then.

In all of his works in this world, Christ always showed how much he loved men, and yet he says one word on the cross by which he does not seem to show himself as being very loving, *Sitio*: "I thirst." For Christ to suffer that strong thirst was a great act of love, but to say that he was suffering it and meaning that they should help him does not seem to have been love. Natural affection, yes, loving affection, no. Someone who tells aloud what he suffers is either seeking relief by communicating it or hoping for it to be resolved through help, and someone who wants his pain reduced or relieved certainly does not have great love for it. Someone who asks for relief from suffering does not wish to suffer; not wishing to suffer is not loving; therefore, Christ's saying *Sitio*, "I thirst," was not an act of love. Let us juxtapose that action of Christ on the cross now with that of Saint Peter on Tabor. Saint Peter's seems to have a great deal of goodness, Christ's does not seem to have any love in it. Can that be how it is?

Two evangelists resolve it with two words. The Evangelist Saint John with a *sciens* and the Evangelist Saint Luke with a *nesciens*. What seemed to be goodness in Saint Peter was not love because it was based on ignorance: *Nesciens quid diceret*.[8] What did not seem to be love in Christ was goodness because it was based on knowledge: *Sciens quia omnia consummata sunt, ut consummaretur scriptura dixit: Sitio*.[9] Let us examine each part. When Saint Peter said *Bonum est nos hic esse*, "not knowing what he said," *Nesciens quid diceret*, it was because he was transported and beside himself. And so, all those cases of goodness that we have considered looked like love and were cases of ignorance. They looked like affection of the will and were errors of understanding. If that resolve of Saint Peter's had been based on a knowledge of the consequences that we have mentioned, there is no doubt that it would have been the most excellent act of love to which the gallantry of a loving heart could attain, but since the resolve was based on ignorance of the very thing he was saying, instead of coming out of it with the title of lover, he came away with the name of fool, because to love without knowing is not loving, it is not knowing.

Not so with Christ, for when he said *Sitio* he knew quite well that since all the other tortures were over, all that was left to be fulfilled was the prophecy of gall; *Sciens quia omni consummata sunt, ut consummaretur scriptura, dixit: Sitio*. Therefore, those moments of weakness that we have considered not seeming to have been love were the greatest of goodnesses. They seem to have been a natural desire and they were the most loving and pure affection. If Christ had said "I thirst" knowing that they would give him water, it would have been asking for relief, but saying "I thirst" knowing that they would give him gall, was asking for more torture. And a love that is ambitious for suffering cannot do more than ask for torture as relief and cure one sorrow by telling them to come forth with another. Christ's saying that he thirsted was not asking for a remedy for his own needs, it was to make others remember their own cruelty, as if he had said: Let me remind you, men, of the gall, which you have forgotten; *Sitio*. Christ's thirst was so different from what it seemed to be. It seemed to be a desire for relief and it was a dropsy of torture. And therefore that knowledge with which Christ worked and the ignorance with which Peter worked reversed the two feelings, so that what looked like goodness in Peter because it was based on ignorance was not love, and what in Christ did not look like love, having been based on knowledge, was goodness. And since knowledge or ignorance is what gives or takes away being and what diminishes or increases the perfection of love, that is why the Evangelist Saint John brings out everything to show what Christ knew in order to prove that he loved: *Sciens quia venit hora ejus, in finem dilexit eos.*[10]

III

Four kinds of ignorance can come together in a lover and greatly diminish the perfection and worthiness of his love: either because he did not know himself, or did not know whom he loved, or did not know love, or did not know the end where the loving would come to rest. If he did not know himself, perhaps he would employ his thought where it would not have been placed if he had known himself. If he did not know whom he loved, perhaps he would be loving with great goodness someone he should have hated if he were not in a state of ignorance. If he did not know love, perhaps he would blindly insist on what he would not have undertaken if he had known what it was. If he did not know the end where the loving would come to rest, perhaps he would come to suffer the harm that he would not have encountered had he foreseen it. All those types of ignorance that are found in men, in Christ were kinds of knowledge and in each and every one the excellence of his extreme love increases. He knew himself, he knew whom he loved, he knew love, and he knew the end where the loving would come to rest. The Evangelist notes it all. He knew himself because he knew that he was no less than God, Son of the Eternal Father: *Sciens quia a Deo exivit.*[11] He knew whom he loved because he knew how ungrateful men were and how cruel they would be to him: *Sciebat enim quisnam esset, qui traderet eum.*[12] He knew love and at great cost to his heart because of the broad experience with which he had loved: *Cum dilexisset suos.*[13] He knew, finally, the end where loving would come to rest, which was death, and what a death: *Sciens quia venit hora ejus.*[14] And with Christ knowing himself, knowing whom he loved, knowing love, and knowing the cruel end he would come to have by loving, would he love nevertheless? A great bounty of love! *In finem dilexit!* In order to know how great and how bountiful it was, let us continue considering each one of these circumstances of knowledge individually.

First, Christ's love was great because he loved us knowing himself: *Sciens quia a Deo exivit.* Christ's knowing himself and loving us is a great and unusual love!

While Paris, ignorant of himself and the fortunes of his birth, stood watch over the sheep of his flock on the pastures of Mount Ida, human history tells us that the object of his interest was Oenone, a rustic beauty of those vales. But when the disguised prince came to know himself and found out that he was the son of Priam, king of Troy, just as he dropped his crook and shepherd's pouch, so, too, he changed his thoughts. He loved humbly as long as he thought himself humble, but as soon as he knew who he was he immediately ceased to know the one he loved. Since that love had been based on ignorance of himself, the same knowledge that undid his ignorance also put an end to the love. The prince ceased to love what the shepherd had loved because, just as it is a lack of knowing themselves for the small to lift up their thoughts, so, too, it is an affront to fate for the great to lower their attention. Oh, prince of glory, it appears that this should have happened to you! But that was not how it was. Anyone who has heard how the Son of God loved us to such extremes could have doubts as to whether the Lord knew himself or lived in ignorance of who he was. In order for the truth of our faith not to be in danger from the extremes of his love and so that the world will not fall into such a mistake, let all know (the Evangelist says) that Christ loved and loved so much, *In finem dilexit*, but let them also know that at the same time he knew who he was: *Sciens quia a Deo exivit.*

If Christ did not know himself, it would have been no great thing for him to love us; but to love us knowing himself went so far beyond that it would seem that the very act of loving us was not knowing himself. The Spouse in the Song of Songs told her Husband once that she loved him with her soul: *Quem diligit anima mea.*[15] And what might he have answered her? *Si ignoras te, o pulcherrima inter mulieres!* "If you do not know yourself, O fairest among women!"[16] A noteworthy reply! So when the Spouse affirms her love to the Husband, the Husband asks the Spouse whether she knows herself: *Si ignoras te.* Discreet and beloved Husband, what kind of an answer is that, and what consequences does that reply of yours contain? When the Spouse assures you of her love, do you doubt that she knows? And when she asserts that she loves you, do you ask her if she does not know herself? *Si ignoras te?* Yes. Because in line with the high esteem in which the Husband holds the merits of the Spouse, to have her affirm that she loved him so much was good reason to doubt that she knew herself. As if the Husband had said, "Do you say you love me?" *Quem dil-igit anima mea?* "Then I say that you do not know yourself." *Si ignoras te, o pulcherrima.* "Because, if you know yourself, how is it possible for you to love me? It was necessary for you to lack knowledge for me to have good fortune to spare. The love for my unworthiness looks very much like igno-rance of your greatness." *Si ignoras te.* "Because if you do not cease know-ing yourself, how can you humble yourself to love me?"

What Solomon said to the Princess of Egypt in ancient times we can say with even more reason to the real Solomon, Christ, in view of the extremes of his love. *Si ignoras te.* Is that love, my God, or ignorance? Do you love us or do you not know yourself? It really seems that you have forgotten who you are and that you have removed yourself from your memory in order to place us in your will. Oh, how high and how deeply did Saint Peter consider those two extremes on this day when, with heavenly surprise, he saw you before him with your knees on the ground: *Tu mihi?* You to me? You to Peter?[17] It seems, Lord, that you neither know yourself nor know me. But the truth is that you know yourself and you love me. And your wisdom in knowing this inequality is as great as your love in bringing those distances together. But in infinite love there well may be room for infinite distances. This is proved by the hands of God next to the feet of men: *Sci-ens quia omnia dedit ei Pater in manus.*[18] Behold the hands of God: *Coepit lavare pedes discipulorum.*[19] Behold the feet of men.

God appeared to Moses in the bush and ordered him to take off his shoes: *Solve calceamenta de pedibus tuis.*[20] When I read that passage I was indeed quite amazed that the majesty and grandeur of God should have anything to do with the feet of Moses. But anyone who casts his eyes on the bush will cease to be amazed at once. The bush in which God appeared was all afire in living flames, and a God wrapped in fire, what a great coun-ter-balance that is to the feet of men! Speaking in our own way, never has God known himself better than when he was in the bush, because there he defined his essence: *Ego sum qui sum.*[21] And as God defined himself, the fire did not go out! With God's knowing himself to the essence, the flames in which he was burning did not diminish! Great love! Defining oneself and turning cold would be weakness; defining oneself and burning, that is loving. God would not have been who he is if he had not loved as he loved. Defining himself was declaring his essence: the burning was proof of the definition. The same thing occurred with Christ on this day: *Sciens quia a Deo exivit, ponit vestimenta sua.* "Knowing that He had come from God He laid aside His garments."[22] The one who knew he was the Son of God knew himself; the one who threw off his clothes was burning; and to know and to burn is love: *In finem dilexit.*

IV

The second ignorance that takes value away from love is the one who loves not knowing the one who is being loved. How many things there are in the world that are loved very much but would become quite despised if the one who loves knew them! The benevolence of deceit and not of love, then. Jacob served Laban for the first seven years and at the end of them, instead of giving him Rachel, they gave him Leah. Oh, deceived shepherd and even more deceived lover! If we were to ask Jacob's imagination for whom he was serving, it would answer Rachel. But if we asked the same question of Laban, who knew what was and what was to be, he would certainly say that Jacob was serving for Leah. And that was how it was. You serve for whom you serve, you do not serve for whom you think. You think that your work and your watching are for Rachel, the loved one, and you work and keep watch for Leah, the despised one. If Jacob had known that he was serving for Leah, he would not have served seven years or seven days. He was serving deceit, then, and not love, because he served for one he did not love. Oh, how many times is that story played out in the theater of the human heart, and with the same figures if not in the same way! The same one that in the imagination is Rachel in reality is Leah, and it is not Laban who is tricking Jacob but Jacob who is tricking himself. Not so the divine lover, Christ. He did not serve for Leah under the imagined figure of Rachel, but he loved Leah known as Leah. Ignorance did not rob him of the value of his love, nor did deceit exchange the object of his work. He loved and suffered for each and every one, not as they ought to be, but just as they were. For his enemy knowing that he was his enemy; for the ingrate knowing that he was an ingrate; and for the traitor knowing that he was a traitor: *Sciebat enim quisnam esset, qui traderet eum.*

From this discourse there follows a conclusion that is as certain as it is unknown, and it is that men do not love what they think they love. Why? Either because what they love is not what they think it is or because they love what is really not there. A person who esteems glass beads thinking them diamonds values diamonds and not glass, a person who loves defects thinking them perfections loves perfections and not defects. You think you love hard diamonds and you love fragile glass. You think you love angelic perfections and you love human imperfections. Therefore, men do not love what they think they love. From that it also follows that they love what really does not exist, because they love things that are not as they are but as they are imagined, and what is imagined and is not does not exist on earth. Not so Christ's love, wise and without deception: *Cum dilexisset suos, qui erant in mundo.*[23]

Take note of the text and its last clause, which seems superfluous and idle—"Having loved his own who were in the world." Well, where were they to be? Outside the world? Of course not. Since it was enough to say "having loved his own," why does the Evangelist add "his own who were in the world, *suos qui erant in mundo*"? It was so that we would understand the knowledge with which Christ loved men, quite different from the way men love. Men love many things that do not exist in the world. They love things as they imagine them, and the things as they imagine them are there in their imagination, but they do not exist in the world. Quite to the contrary, Christ loved men as they truly were in the world and not as they might deceptionally be in the imagination: *Cum dilexisset suos, qui erant in mundo.* Christ did not love his own as you love your own. You love them as they are in your imagination and not as they are in the world. In the world they are ingrates, in your imagination they are thankful; in the world they are enemies, in your imagination they are friends. And loving your enemy thinking he is your friend and the traitor thinking he is loyal and the ingrate thinking he is grateful is not goodness, it is ignorance. Therefore, your love has no value; it is nothing but deception. Only Christ's was true love and true goodness because he loved his own as they were and with complete knowledge of what they were—the enemy, knowing his hate, the ingrate, knowing his ingratitude, and the traitor, knowing his disloyalty: *Sciebat enim quisnam esset, qui traderet eum.*

But if that knowledge of Christ was universal with regards to all his disciples (who were his own who were in the world), why does the Evangelist make particular note of that same knowledge with respect to Judas, telling us that the Lord knew who the one was who would hand him over? *Sciebat enim quisnam esset, qui traderet eum.* Christ knew Judas as completely as Peter and the others, but the Evangelist makes special note of the Lord's knowledge with respect to Judas because in Judas, more than in any of the others, he displayed the goodness of his love. See now. Defining good love Saint Bernard says, *Amor non quaerit causam, nec fructum*: "Good love seeks neither cause nor fruit." [24] If I love because I am loved, the love has a cause, if I love so that I will be loved, it has fruit, and good love should not have a because or a for which. If I love because I am loved, it is an obligation, I am doing what I must do; if I love so that I will be loved, it is a negotiation, I am looking for what I desire. So how should one love for it to be good? *Amo, quia amo, amo ut amem*: I love because I love and I love in order to love. One who loves because he is loved is thankful, one who loves so he will be loved is self-seeking; one who loves not because he is loved or so he will be loved, he alone shows good love. And such was Christ's goodness with regard to Judas, based on the knowledge he had of him and of the other disciples.

In the course of that last supper Christ said to his disciples: *Jam non dicam vos servos, sed amicos*. "No longer do I call you servants, but friends."[25] With things being thus, read all the Gospels and you will find that he only called Judas friend when he said *Amice, ad quid venisti?* Well, Lord, was not Peter there, was not John there, more than all deserving of the name of friend? Why do you not give them that name instead of Judas? Judas the enemy? Judas the falsifier? Judas the traitor given the name of friend? *Amice?!* On this day, yes. Because Christ on this day was not looking for reasons for love, he was looking for the circumstances for goodness. Christ knew that the other disciples loved him and he knew that they would love him to the point of giving their lives for him. Because they loved him his love had cause, and because they were to love him it had fruit. On the contrary, Judas did not love Christ because he sold him, nor was he to love him because he was to persist in his obstinacy unto death; and for the Lord to love someone who did not love him and never would love him was to love without cause and without fruit and therefore was the greatest goodness. To love known ingratitude is something that is sometimes found in love. But nobody has loved a known ingratitude who at the same time did not love expected thanks. Only Christ was so good and so loving that he loved without correspondence, because he loved someone he knew did not love him and would never love him. Therefore, he gives the title of friend only to Judas not because love was deserved, but because he believed in goodness. To love for reasons of love is done by all, but to love for reasons of hate is only done by Christ. He made obligations out of offenses and reasons out of affronts because it was an obligation of his love to reach the greatest goodness: *In finem dilexit*.

V

The third circumstance of knowledge that greatly enhanced Christ's love was the knowledge he had of love itself. Christ knew all things with the three highest knowledges: with divine knowledge as God, with holy knowledge as a chosen one, with ingrained knowledge as the leader of mankind and the Redeemer of the world. He even knew love with a fourth knowledge, which was the one acquired from experience, because just as Saint Paul says that he learned to obey by suffering, so, too, he learned to love by loving. And that is what Saint John pondered at length, stating that "having loved, he loved." *Cum dilexisset, dilexit.*

A curious question in this philosophy is which is the most precious and has the most perfections, the first love or the second? No one can deny of the first that it is the firstborn of the heart, the heir to affection, the flower of desire, and the first fruit of the will. Nonetheless, I can recognize great advantages in the second love. The first is untutored, the second is experienced; the first is an apprentice, the second a master; the first can be drive, the second can only be love. In short, the second, because it is the second, is the confirmation and ratification of the first and, therefore, not simple love, but duplicated, love upon love. It is true that the first is the firstborn of the heart; the will that is always free, however, does not have its possessions entailed. It may be the first, but it is not the greatest because of that.

The first time that Jonathan felt affection for David, the Holy Scripture says he swore an oath of everlasting love: *Inierunt autem David et Jonathas foedus; diligebat enim eum, quasi animam suam.*[27] After that they passed some time with strong wills but varying fortune. The text goes on to say that Jonathan swore another oath to David that he would never go back on his love: *Et addidit Jonathas dejerare David, eo quod diligeret illum.*[28] Well, if Jonathan had already taken an oath to love David, why does he take another now? Could he possibly have broken the first so that a second was necessary? It is certain that he had not broken it because Jonathan was not only the finest example of friendship but also of steadfastness. So if his love had been sworn to in the beginning, why does he swear to it again now? Because it was quite a different matter to swear to love before it is known than it is to swear to it after it has been experienced. When Jonathan swore the first time he did not know what it was to love because he had not experienced it. When he swore the second time he already had a broad experience of what it was and what it cost from all that he had suffered for David, and the concept that Jonathan now had of one love and the other led him to judge that the oath of the first did not oblige him to keep the second. Therefore, so that his past ignorance should not diminish the present value, he swore a new oath of love. Not new because he may have ceased to love at some time, but because what he had promised before was little in comparison to the much that he loved today. Then he promised from what he knew, now he was promising from what he had experienced. Jonathan's deciding to love David when he did not know the passion of that tyrannical affection was not great goodness, but after knowing its rigors, after suffering its injustices, after experiencing its cruelties, after being subject to its tyrannies, after feeling absences, after resisting contradictions, after stumbling through difficulties, after overcoming impossibilities, risking his life, spurning his honor, pulling down authority, revealing secrets, covering truths, uncovering spies, surrendering his soul, subjecting his wishes, checking his free will, dying inside from torture and living in his friend through care, always sad, always afflicted, always restless, always faithful, in spite of his father and the fortune of them both (all these acts of goodness Jonathan does for David as Scripture says), after, I say, such qualified experiences of his heart and his love, he decided a second time to take an oath of eternal love. That, yes, that is love!

I say the same of our good Lover, with the advantage that the Son of God has over the son of Saul. If Christ had been able not to know love, or had not known it through experience, his loving us would have been less. Having known love through experience, however, and knowing that his own love was so rigorous that it drew him out of his father's breast, that it was so inhuman that it sent him forth on earth in a manger, that it was so cruel that a week after his birth it drew the blood from his veins, that it was so unloving that before he was two months old it exiled him for seven years in Egypt, and it was so tyrannical that if it did not take away his life at the hands of Herod it was because it was not content with so little blood, with Christ knowing that this was his love, he did not desist or repent but, rather, continued loving, a great love! Great because he loved, but very much greater because he loved upon having loved: *Cum dilexisset, dilexit*.

I can see quite well that theologians will answer me by saying that Christ's love from the first instant until the last was always the same and never grew. That is what reason demands. If love's diminishing discredits it, so, too, does its growing. Anyone who says he loves more discredits his love because even though the growth is increase it is an increase that supposes imperfection. Love that can grow is not a perfect love. So if Christ's most perfect love was always the same and never grew, how can we say that it was greater on this day? They would all reply, and quite well, that it was greater in its effects. But unrefined that I am, in the very substance of love, I still cannot help recognizing some consideration of its being greater. I confess that it did not grow, but it could well be greater without growing. A column on its base, a statue on a pedestal grows without growing. That was how Christ's love was on this day, because it was love on top of love. And just as the base and the pedestal were of the same substance, so the same substance of Christ's love is not only higher today, but, in a certain way, greater. So much so that in my view the words of the Evangelist can have no other meaning: *Cum dilexisset, dilexit*, "As he had loved, he loved." These words say more than they seem. "Had loved" and "loved" have no difference except in tense; there is no distinction in meaning. What, then, is the Evangelist telling us new? If he had said "as he had loved much, now he loved more," it would have been well; that is what he wanted to prove. But if he wanted to say that he loved more, how is it that he only said he loved? Because he said it in such terms that by saying only that he loved, it remains proven that he loved more: *Cum dilexisset, dilexit*, "As he had loved, he loved," and the matter of loving on top of having loved is not only loving afterwards, but loving more. It not only speaks of a relationship in time but an excess of love. And since the Evangelist wanted to raise up the great amount that the Lord loved on this day, he understood that in order to enhance the present love it was enough to put it on top of the past.

When God ordered Abraham to sacrifice his son with all the severity of the Hebraic character, the text reads thus: *Tolle filium tuum, quem dilexisti Isaac*. "Take now your son Isaac, whom you loved."[29] "Whom you love" seems to be what he should have said, because God's whole intent was to exalt the love in order to make the sacrifice more difficult. So why did he not say "sacrifice to me the son whom you love" rather than "the son whom you loved"? For that very reason. God wanted to exalt the love in order to make the sacrifice more difficult and there is no way in which present love can be exalted more than to imagine it past. Sacrifice to me not only the son that you love but the one that you loved, because loving upon having loved is the greatest love. That is why the Evangelist on this day, comparing love with love, does not make a comparison between great and excessive, but between first and second: *Cum dilexisset, dilexit*. This was the first and second wound of the heart of which our divine Lover, long before love shot its arrows at him, was already glorifying in: *Vulnerasti cor meum, soror mea sponsa, vulnerasti cor meum.*[30] The first wound was that of past love, the second that of present love, and for proof of which was greater and more penetrating, if it is not enough to be wounded on top of a wound, let it be sufficient to know that with the first he lived and that the second took his life away: *Cum dilexisset, in finem dilexit.* And we have arrived, without intending to, at the fourth consideration.

VI

The fourth and final circumstance in which Christ's knowledge refined the extremes of his love very much was knowing and being aware of the end he was to come to loving: *Sciens quia venit hora ejus.* Stories are told of many people who died because they loved, but because love was only the occasion and ignorance the cause, death falsely gave them the epitaph of lovers. A lover is not one who dies because he loved, but one who loved in order to die. Quite noteworthy in this type is the example of Prince Sichem. Sichem loved Dinah, the daughter of Jacob, and he gave in to the demands of her affection to such a degree that, although a sovereign prince, he subjected himself to such conditions and expedients that after a few days of marriage Simeon and Levi, Dinah's brothers, were able to take his life. Sichem loved and he died; but death was not a trophy of his love, it was a punishment for his ignorance. It was an event and not a reward because he did not love in order to die, even though he died because he loved. Dinah owed him love but she did not owe him death; or rather, she did not even owe him love, since one who loved because he did not know that he was about to die, if he knew it, would not have loved. The merit of love is not in death, but in the knowledge of it.

See it clearly in Abraham and Isaac. During those three days in which Abraham was walking to the hill of sacrifice with his son Isaac, both were going along in equal danger because one was going to die and the other was going to kill or kill himself, but they were not going in equal goodness because one knew where he was walking and the other did not. The road was the same, the steps were equal, but the knowledge was quite different and, therefore, the value as well. Abraham deserved much, Isaac did not deserve anything, because Abraham was walking along with knowledge, Isaac with ignorance, Abraham to the known sacrifice, Isaac to the unknown sacrifice. That is the difference between Christ's sacrifice and all those sacrificed by death because of love. Only Christ went voluntarily to a known death, all the others unwillingly to an unknown death. Sichem, Samson,

Amnon, and the others who died because they loved were carried off to death by love with their eyes blindfolded like condemned men. Only Christ, triumphant, had his eyes open. (I could have used more honorable antitheses, but these are the ones that we read about in Scripture.) Sichem would not have loved Dinah, nor Samson Delilah, nor Amnon Tamar if they had foreseen the death that awaited them. Only Christ's knowledge knew that this love was leading him to death and only Christ, knowing it and seeing it coming for him, walked courageously to meet it: *Sciens quia venit hora ejus.*

How well and how poetically did David sing of him: *Sol cognovit occasum suum,* "The sun knows its going down."[31] A few words, but difficult ones. The Sun is an irrational and unfeeling creature. (Because even though some philosophers believed the contrary, it is a condemned error.) So if the Sun has no understanding or feelings, how can the Prophet say that the Sun knew its setting? *Sol cognovit occasum suum.* What is certain (Augustine says) is that beneath the metaphor of the material Sun, David was speaking of the divine Sun, Christ, who is the only Sun with understanding. And because both were very much alike in hastening toward their setting, that is why he portrayed the subtleties of one with the insensibilities of the other. If the light of the Sun were the true light of knowledge and the west where the Sun goes to set were true death, would it not cause us great surprise to see that the Sun, knowing the place of its death, hastened to the west with the same speed with which it climbs to its zenith? Well, that is what that divine Sun did: *Sol cognovit occasum suum.* The divine Sun truly knew its setting because it knew specifically the hour in which, reaching the final horizons of life, it was to pass from this to the other hemisphere: *Sciens quia venit hora ejus, ut transeat ex hoc mundo.* And that with that certain knowledge of the cruel end to which its love was leading it, it would walk without taking a step backwards just as sprightly to the true and known setting as the material Sun itself, which neither dies nor knows. A great resolution of the bravery of love! Not only knowing death and going to die but going to die, knowing it, as if it did not!

Only Saint John, who gave us the thought, may have the proof. When his enemies came to take Christ, the Evangelist says: *Sciens omnia quae ventura erant super meum, processit, et dixit: quem quaeritis?* "Knowing all things that would come upon Him, [he] went forward and said to them, "Whom are you seeking?"[32] It seems to be incompatible with the terms of this narration. A person who knows does not ask. If Christ knew everything, then, and knew that they were looking for him, and the Evangelist notes that he knew, why does he ask as if he did not know? The reason and the mystery is because from that point on Christ was beginning to walk toward death and that was the way in which his love was leading him. It was leading him to death knowing as if it were leading him not knowing. Anyone reading what the Evangelist says will say that Christ knew. Anyone who hears what Christ asks will think that Christ did not know. And in both truth and in appearance that was all. In truth he knew and in appearance he did not know, because he loved in such a way that he went to die knowing as if he loved and died not knowing.

That is the secret that was covered by that veil or that mysterious eclipse with which love on this day covered the eyes of Christ in the hands of his enemies: *Velaverunt eum et percutiebant faciem ejus.* I am not surprised that the Lord suffered many other tortures because one who loves above all else offers himself up for everything. But to allow them to cover his eyes seems not only to offend his patience but much more his love. Did not Saint John on this day with that repeated *sciens* take off the blindfold from Christ's love so that the world would know that he loved with his eyes open? Because that was the skill with which Christ's love knew how to make one confuse knowledge and ignorance. It made him love in such a way with his eyes open as he would have loved with his eyes closed. That he loved in such a way knowing as he would have loved not knowing. Love freed itself of that veil that seemed an affront and avenged itself with greater honor than Saint John had done it. Saint John took the blindfold off Christ's love and that same love put it back on Christ so that we would notice that he loved in such a way knowing and with his eyes closed: *Velaverunt eum.* Christ knew himself and he loved as if he did not know. He knew what he loved and he loved as if he had not experienced it. He foresaw the end he was to reach loving and he loved as if he had not foreseen it. And because he loved knowing as if he had loved not knowing, that was why only he loved and knew how to love with goodness: *Sciens, sciens, sciens, in finem dilexit eos.*

VII

We have considered Christ's love through the remarks of Saint John. Let us consider it now through the remarks of Christ himself, which, as coming from the one who knew it best, will be the most pondered and profound. We have the contest on this day between the greatest lover and the greatest loved one—Christ and Saint John—a contest, I say, in exalting the extremes of that very love, and after Saint John said what he knew, remarking that Christ loved knowing: "Now (Christ says) this is not the greatest circumstance that elevates the high point of my love. If men wish to know the goodness with which I love them, they should not ponder my knowledge, they should ponder their ignorance. I loved men very much because I loved them knowing everything, but my love was much greater because as I loved them they did not know how much I loved them: *Quod ego facio, tu nescis.*" No matter how much men make speeches and elevate their thoughts, they will never come to know the love with which Christ loved them, neither how much as God nor how much as man, and that Christ has resolved to love not only those who do not return his love, but those who do not even know it! That my love is not to enjoy the satisfaction of repayment, and not even the relief of knowledge! That was the greatest valor of Christ's loving heart and that was the greatest difficulty because it broke the strength of his love.

Therefore let us ask this question: What is most desired and most esteemed by love? To see itself known or to see itself repaid? It is certain that love cannot be repaid without first being known, but it can be known without being repaid. And, thinking about these two terms separately, there is no doubt that love esteems more and prefers to see itself known more than repaid, because what love seeks most is obligation; knowledge obliges, repayment releases. Therefore it is much better for love to see itself known than repaid, because knowledge tightens obligations, repayment and release loosen them. Knowledge is the satisfaction of one's own love, repayment is the satisfaction of another's love. In the satisfaction received by love there can be an interested affection, the satisfaction that is communicated can only be liberal. Therefore, love should esteem more having the secure knowledge of the satisfaction of its liberality than looking doubtfully upon the nobility of its disinterest. The most secure credit of one who loves is the confession of debt on the part of the loved one, but how can one confess the debt who does not know it? More important for love, therefore, is knowledge, not repayment, because its greatest wealth is always having the beloved in one's debt. When love ceases to be a creditor, only then is it poor. Finally, when the love is so great that it cannot be repaid, it is the greatest glory of the one who loves. If that greatness is known, it is a manifest glory; if it is not known, it remains in the dark and is not glory. Therefore, much more esteemed and much more desired is love for the glory of being known than the satisfaction of being repaid. Enough of reasoning, let us turn to Scripture.

The greatest deed of human love was that courageous resolution with which the Prophet Abraham, placing divine love before natural and parental love, decided to take the life of his own son. God laid his hand on the sword of his unloving and most loving servant, and what he told him immediately was: *Nunc cognovi quod timeas Deum.*[34] "Now I know, Abraham, that you love me." That is what *timeas* in the phrase from Scripture means, and that is how many translate it and all interpret it: *Nunc cognovi quod diligis Deum.*[35] After this a large ram appeared there, caught in some brambles, who gave a happy ending to the unimagined sacrifice, and when it was over God spoke again to Abraham and said to him: *Quia fecisti hanc rem, benedicam tibi et multiplicabo semen tuum sicut stellas coeli.* "Because you have done this thing, I will bless you and I will multiply your descendants as the stars of the heaven" and the Messiah shall be born of you.

This was the case as it happened. Let us now take a good look at it. God spoke twice to Abraham here and he told him two things: one immediately when he held back his sword and the other afterwards. What he told him immediately was that he knew that Abraham loved him: *Nunc cognovi quod diligis Deum.* What he told him afterwards was that he would liberally reward that action: *Quia fecisti rem hanc,* etc. Therefore, I ask, why does God tell Abraham in the first place that he knew his love and in the second that he would reward it? And, since he delayed for afterwards the promise of reward, why did he not also delay the recognition of his knowledge, *Nunc cognovi?* God spoke as one who knows hearts and knows what one who truly loves esteems most. First, he made Abraham aware that he knew his love and he kept for later his assuring him that he was to be rewarded, because, as Abraham was such a true and fine lover, he would rather see his love known than repaid. The promise of reward was therefore delayed, but the revelation of knowledge was given immediately and at the same moment. Because a great love can more easily suffer the delay or hopes of repayment than the doubts of being known. First, I say that the consequence of God's telling Abraham that he knew his love when he commanded him to withhold his sword was necessary because if Abraham had not known for certain that his love was already known, without doubt he would have struck the blow so that the blood of the best part of his heart would have shouted out how truly he loved. And since love wants, above all, to see itself known, and since men do not know the love of Christ (or rather, since it is impossible to know it as it is), his love overcomes that difficulty and rides over that impossibility and, in spite of it and of himself, he loved, a stupendous resolve of love!

VIII

Loving us cost Christ a great deal, and he suffered a great deal as he loved us. The harshest pain that his love condemned him to, however, was that he loved those who did not know him. This is what a person who loves feels most and what injures him most. Two faints or two great accidents are suffered by the Spouse in the Song of Songs, both caused by her love. One was in the beginning, which is written in Chapter 2, the other was after having loved much and is mentioned in Chapter 5. There was for the Spouse, however, a difference worthy of great consideration and note in these two accidents. In the first incident she said: *Fulcite me floribus, stipate me malis, quia amore langueo.*[37] "Sustain me with comforts, bring me roses and flowers, for I am lovesick." In the second she says: *Adjuro vos, filiae Jerusalem, si inveneritis dilectum, ut nuntietis ei, quia amore langueo.* "I charge you, O daughters of Jerusalem, if you find my beloved, that you tell him I am lovesick!"[38] A noteworthy difference! If the Spouse in both cases was equally ill with love, *quia amore langueo*, for what reason in the first incident did she ask for cures and comforts and not in the second? And if in the second she did not think of asking for cures, why does she call upon her friends with such entreaty and ask them to swear they will let her Husband know? *Adjuro vos, ut nuntietis dilecto.* The truth of what we are saying could not be better painted. In the first incident, in which the Spouse was still a beginner in love, she only asked for cures for the illness because the painful effects that her heart felt were the ones that hurt most. In the second incident, however, in which love was already perfect and fulfilled, instead of saying for them to come with cures for her ailment, she says for them to go with news to her Beloved for her pain did not hurt her as much because she was suffering it as because he was unaware of it. The Spouse attended first to what hurt her most, and the affects of her love hurt her more because the object was unaware of them than because the subject suffered them. Therefore, instead of saying, Bring me a cure, she said, Take him news. The pains of her love afflicted her much more because of his not knowing than because they were suffered! It was the same with Christ.

In Psalm 34, according to the Greek text, the Son of God has this to say: *Congregata sunt super me flagella, et ignoraverunt.* "Scourgers gathered against me, and they did not know." For understanding of this affection we must suppose that of all the tortures of his passion, Christ did not feel any as much as the lashes. Reason would be enough proof, but the Lord himself so declared when he revealed to his disciples what he was about to suffer: *Tradetur gentibus, et iludetur, et flagellabitur, et conspuetur, et postquam flagellaverint, occident eum.*[40] Of all the other tortures and of death itself he spoke only once. The torture of the lashes, however, he repeated twice, *Flagellabitur et postquam flagellaverint,* because what the heart feels most naturally comes out of the mouth more times. The Lord then says: *Congregata sunt super me flagella, et ignoraverunt.* "Scourgers gathered against me, and they did not know." Afflicted Jesus, what manner of terms are these? If the lashes were the torture most felt by you, it would seem that you should have said: "The lashes fell upon me. Oh, how I felt them! Oh, how they tormented me!" But instead of saying that he felt them and they tormented him, the Lord complained only that they did not know, because in the midst of the greatest excesses of his love, what most tormented Christ's heart was not that he was suffering, but that men did not know: *Et ignoraverunt.* He does not complain of the lashes and he does complain of the ignorance, because the lashes are an affront to the person, ignorance discredits love. And one who loved to such an extreme that he tried to purchase the credits of his love at the price of the affronts to his person saw in the end his person affronted and the love not known, oh, what insufferable grief! And because that lack of knowledge is what one who loves feels most and should feel most, therefore Christ pondered the goodness of his love, not through the circumstance of his knowledge, but through that of our ignorance: *Quod ego facio, tu nescis.*[41] Christ's love is elevated much more by that *nescis* than by Saint John's *sciens,* repeated so many times. Because if they were great circumstances of love, to love knowing oneself and knowing whom one loved and knowing love and knowing where it was all to end, loving, above all these considerations there rises up and incomparably stands above the use of all that knowledge and all that love for those who would not know it: *Tu nescis.*

IX

But in matters like that men's ignorance was, on the one side, the greatest feeling, and, on the other, the greatest credit of Christ's love. The love itself made such delicate use of it that it took that same ignorance as the instrument to give credit to us without concern for the consequences that might discredit it. When Christ was raised to the Cross, that is, to the throne of his love in its most public theater, which was Calvary, the first words he spoke were these: *Pater dimitte illis, non enim sciunt quid faciunt.* "Father, forgive them, for they do not know what they do."[42] For they do not know what they do, O loving Pardoner? And does your love know what it obliges you to do by the reason that you cite? If our ignorance makes us less ungrateful, it also makes you less of a lover because love sharpens his arrows on the stone of ingratitude and the longer it lasts the more he sharpens them. How can you form, therefore, excuses for our ingratitude from which you could make reasons for your acts of goodness sprout? I thought I had told you already of the greatest of them all, but this one was the greatest. Christ went as far as to diminish the credit of his love in order to disguise and cover up the defects of ours, and he tried to appear as less of a lover only so that we could seem less ungrateful. That was how he used men's ignorance, with the consideration of our ignorance being the most subtle reason for his goodness.

But for that very reason it came to be otherwise, and where Christ's love risked its good opinion it emerged with even more belief. Because a lover cannot arrive at any greater goodness than esteeming the credit of his loved one more than the credit of his love. An example of such excellence can only be found in Christ himself.

Christ was born in a manger and says through the mouth of the Evangelist that he was born there "because there was no room for them in the inn": *Quia non erat ei locus in diversorio.*[43] Holy Evangelist, do not say such a thing! That might have been the occasion, but that was not the cause. Christ was born in a manger because he loved men so much that he wanted to suffer that lack of shelter for them, and he was born outside the city because men were so hard and ungrateful that they did not wish to give him shelter in Bethlehem. Well, then, if Christ's love and men's ingratitude were the cause, why is Christ's worthiness not mentioned and the blame, which belonged to men, is attributed to the occasion and the time: *Quia non erat ei locus in diversorio*? What is certain is that Christ showed himself more the lover in the cause that he pointed out than in the lack of shelter he suffered. He wanted what was his choice to appear as necessity and what was our ingratitude to appear as contingency, so that in that contingency ingratitude would be disguised and in the necessity love. The ingratitude increased the goodness, the necessity decreased the love, and Christ wished to seem less of a lover so that men would appear less ungrateful. That was how he loved at the beginning of his life and that was how he ended when it was over. That is why he forgives men's ingratitude because of their ignorance, *Non enim sciunt quid faciunt*, men's ignorance being the greatest credit of his love: *Quod ego facio, tu nescis.*

X

This was, Christians, Christ's love, this was the knowledge and the kinds of knowledge with which he loved us, and this was the ignorance and the kinds of ignorance over which we are loved. Let us carry always before our eyes that *sciens* and that *nescis*. Let us keep always in our memory (which the Lord himself recommended so much to us on this day) his knowledge and our ignorance. Let his knowledge serve us as an awakener so that we will never cease to love. Let our ignorance serve us as a stimulus so that we will love more and more the one who loved us so much. How can we not always love the one who is always seeing us and knowing if we love him? How can we not love very much the one who loved us so much that we will never be able to grasp or know it?

Oh, how great will our confusion be if we consider well the strength and correspondence of that *sciens* and that *nescis*! When Christ asked Saint Peter so many times if he loved him, the latter replied, astonished at the question: *Tu, Domine, scis quia amo te.* "Yes, Lord; You know that I love You."[44] Compare now that *tu scis* of Peter's spoken to Christ with the *tu nescis* of Christ spoken to Peter. When Christ loves Peter, Peter does not know how much Christ loves him: *Tu nescis*. But when Peter loves Christ, Christ knows how much Peter loves him: *Tu scis*. Oh, such a notable disproportion of love and knowledge! Peter's love known, Christ's love not known. Christ's love suffers our ignorance, ours suffers his knowledge, and both can be equally complaining. Christ's complaining because men do not know it, *Tu nescis*, men's complaining because Christ knows it: *Tu scis*. If Christ did not know men's love, our love would have consolation in its frailty, and if men knew Christ's love, his love would have satisfaction in its excess. But with Christ's love being so excessive, men cannot know it! And men's love being so imperfect, Christ knows it! Very equal and very unequal is the fate of both. The remedy for that, Lord, would be for you and us to exchange hearts. If you loved us with our hearts, the love and merit would be equal and our ignorance would be enough to recognize it; and if we loved you with yours, we would love you as you deserved and only your knowledge would know our love. But since this cannot be, you, as the only one who knows yourself, must love yourself; you, as the only one who knows your love, must repay it. And let the only glory due you and your love be the knowing that only by you can it be repaid and only by you can it be known. That is what we believe, that is what we confess, and, prostrate at the feet of your love, we offer it an eternal crown woven from that *nescis* and that *sciens*: *Sciens quia venit hora ejus, in finem dilexit eos.*

Letter to King Afonso VI
From the Shores of Cumá on May 22, 1661

Sire – the priests of the Society of Jesus in Maranhão, missionaries in Your Majesty's service, have been driven out of Indian villages and removed from their Chapter House and held prisoner in a secular house, in addition to other affronts and violence unworthy of having been committed by Catholics and subjects of Your Majesty.

The ones who brought this action about were the people, so-called, but the ones who motivated and captivated and gave the people the drive to do this are those about whom I have already warned Your Majesty many times, those who most should have defended the cause of the Faith, the spread of Christianity, and obedience to and obeisance of Your Majesty's laws.

The sole inner and encompassing reason behind this resolve, as it has been pondered for quite some time, is greed, especially that of those most powerful; and because they are not content with what they are allowed by Your Majesty's laws, and there are no others left to defend these laws and freedom and justice for the Indians but the priests of the Society of Jesus, they have resolved finally to rid themselves of this impediment by dastardly means. I kept on telling them that if they were not satisfied they should turn to Your Majesty, as author and master of the laws, and that Your Majesty, once all parties have been heard, would revoke or confirm what might be just, but they mistrusted your justice and never wished to accept such reason.

The motives for this last step, so that it might be brought about, as the Governor has written me, were the three following reasons.

First: for making public in this State the letter I wrote Your Majesty about what had been done to these missions in the year 1659, which Your Majesty ordered printed; and it is difficult to believe how much this letter aroused those who cannot bear, after having been so many years in this State, these things that had never been done until the arrival of priests of the Society.

Second: there also arrived in Maranhão and were published some letters I wrote Your Majesty through the Bishop of Japan, in which I reported
to Your Majesty of the contradictions there were in this State concerning
the propagation of the Faith and how badly Your Majesty's laws concerning justice for the Indians are followed, about which Your Majesty had
repeatedly ordered me to report through the Bishop and and to point out
the measures that might be taken to help them. And because I did that,
naming among those who broke the laws the Carmelite brothers, whose
Provincial, Friar Estêvão da Natividade, was the first to break them, this
same Provincial, sailing to Portugal on the ship that also bore the letters
and was captured by Dunkirk corsairs, schemed to lay hands on them, and
he held them in secret until the death of the Bishop, and then he turned
them over to his monks, who published them, and thus was brought about
what publicly and secretly they had many times attempted to do.

Third: the imprisonment of the Indian Lopo de Sousa Guarapaúba.
This Indian is the chieftain of a village and after the publication of Your
Majesty's laws he never sought to follow them and, protected by powerful
people, for whom he therefore did many services, as he and his people all
the while lived a heathen life, having been Christians for quite some time,
because, although this chieftain had many mistresses, he had been married
in facie Ecclesiae to the sister of another woman with whom he publicly
had children before he married, keeping this impediment quiet and intim-
idating all the people in the village so that no one would reveal it, allowing
them to live in the same manner, not attending mass or keeping any sacrament, not even at the hour of death, so that all of them were dying without confession and in a state of sin; in short, heathens in every way and
disobeying Your Majesty's laws, against which this Chieftain was captur-
ing free Indians and selling them as slaves, and there were others he killed
according to heathen ceremonies, and all of this was tolerated by those
who should have punished him and for the vilest of motives. This Chieftain was already admonished many times by the priests for the excesses
mentioned above and especially those having to do with the Church, but
there was no improvement whatever. So, without recourse to any gentler
measures, I proposed to the Governor that it would be most proper for this
Indian to be punished as an example to the rest, who were already claiming
him and using him as an excuse, which the Governor did not wish to do,
telling me that it would be better if we punished him through the Church,
and he gave orders for me to have the soldiers needed for his arrest, and
that the Captain-General of Pará supply them, and that was why he was

arrested, while the uprising in the village was not spontaneous, as was falsely reported, but rather caused by many people, ecclesiastic and lay as well as ministers of Your Majesty, who persuaded the Indians to rise up.

These three reasons, so justified they say, were the ultimate cause of what has been done, but the true cause, Sire, is what I have told Your Majesty: the insatiable greed of those at the top, which, in this very same year, before these other events took place, had already brought on uprisings, both in Maranhão and in Pará. In Maranhão they insisted that women, as well as their husbands, were to be distributed among the settlers for their use, against Your Majesty's laws; and in Pará they held an auction, beyond the time and occasion allowed by the laws, threatening that if it was not consented to, they would do it on their own account, and they drew up papers to gather the people together, and all the rest.

Now, they say, they are sending investigators to this governance, and they are picking up Indians who are their close associates and who, because of the abominable lives they lead, do not want doctrine and subjection to the priests; and all will say and bear witness in writing and swear against the truth whatever passion dictates to them, along with hatred and unjust blind interest. So that, Sire, because we hold to Your Majesty's laws, and because we tell Your Majesty of the excesses by which these are disdained, and because we defend freedom and justice for the miserable Christian Indians and those who at this moment are being proselytized, and most of all because we are a hindrance to the sins and injustices that used to be committed in this State, we are insulted, arrested, and cast out.

Our only regret (for otherwise we would give infinite thanks to God) is the ruination of so many thousands of souls, and of the successful beginnings of such a flourishing Christianity, which, because of these measures, is being destroyed and falling apart, with the loss of all that until now had been brought about and attained with such effort; because the whole reason for the conversion of heathen Indians, peace with those who had been enemies, and the coming to us of those who were lost in the jungle, with their accepting the Faith and obedience to the Church, had been the promise to them in the name of Your Majesty that they would be under the protection of the priests, whom they have seen to be the only ones defending them; and this example now has caused a loss of belief in our word, of the authority of Your Majesty's laws and the promises that we made them in Your Majesty's name; in a word, of everything.

Of everything I have told Your Majesty I received word while at sea where I am writing this, coming to Maranhão from a visit to the Christians in Pará and along the Amazon River, where I had lately established two missions, one for the Tapajó nation and the other for the Nheengaíbas, who, according to what has been promised, are coming out of the forests and have already set up nine villages along the banks of the rivers. Even the nations that have dealings with the Dutch at present have sent word asking us to accept them as our children under the same conditions of peace and as vassals of Your Majesty. But while the heathen barbarians are doing all this, the Portuguese and the religious people detain and deport us, and this in the towns of our most Catholic king and the kingdom that God has chosen for him for the propagation of His Faith.

For that reason, Sire, I have abandoned the route I had been taking to Maranhão and I return to Pará and the Amazon River to see if I can in some way save this part of Christ's flock and confirm the Indians who with this case are all now finding themselves under their former slavery and tyranny, so that they do not after being baptized return to the forests and heathendom, and also, Sire, to lift the spirits of the priests of the Society, who, having left the ease and quiet of their homelands and Colleges, are leading quite different lives now, seeing themselves subject to these turmoils and persecutions, not suffered for the Faith (which they would regard quite highly), but because of the disobedience and scant Christianity of Your Majesty's vassals and ministers.

Of the few that we are, four priests have died this year, all in the countryside working with the Indians and their conversion and with a complete lack of any human things, and while we were so constantly serving God and Your Majesty, whose missionaries we are, let Your Majesty judge, Sire, if it is just that we should suffer for this cause, and if the justice of it should not be under the protection of Your Majesty's royal arm.

All we ask for our part, prostrate at Your Majesty's royal feet, for the blood of Jesus Christ, are the two following things rightfully owed everyone.

1st. For Your Majesty to order at once the restoration and reinvestment of the priests of the Society to the position they previously held, in their College as well as in all the Indian villages, with the same authority and jurisdiction that they possessed before and of which they were so unjustly, violently, dangerously, and sacrilegiously deprived. Also that there be no rebuttal or doubt in this, allowing no petition by the inhabitants of this State concerning this restitution.

2nd. That after this restitution is done, Your Majesty not allow any proposal whatever by said inhabitants be resolved without first my being heard. And I say my being heard, Sire, because I was the one who organized this mission by Your Majesty's order, and I have taken part in all the preparations, so only I have the underlying knowledge of everything and only I can inform you and put forth the reasons for the details and the great damage that it underwent.

Finally, recalling and laying before Your Majesty two other conditions of great import for the first resolution of this matter and the speed with which it must be done.

1st. Let the laws and government which the inhabitants of Maranhão reject be consulted in a meeting of the most prominent legal men in the kingdom, then let be heard the Procurators of Maranhão and Pará, with a decree from Your Majesty, as requested by me, that they agree to everything that might be legal and possible in good conscience; and let this be done. From which it will follow that everything else that they claim be illegal and unjust.

2nd. That the Tobajara highland Indians and the Tobajaras and Potigoaras taken out of Pernambuco, and the Jurunas and the Nheengaíbas, and the Anajazes, and the Mapuazes, and the Mamaianás, and the Aruans, and the Poquis, and the Poucigoaras, and the Tupinambás, which are the nations recently brought into the Faith by the priests of the Society, and many others they are currently bringing in; to all those nations it was professed and promised in Your Majesty's name that thay would not be under the immediate subjection of the Portuguese settlers but under the rule of their Chieftains and the protection of the Society, which, according to Your Majesty's laws, was to defend them from the former oppressions they suffered. And under this condition and the others contained in the aforementioned laws of the last Decree by Your Majesty, they accepted and swore to peace, obedience, and the vassalage in which Your Majesty holds them. And if now the aforesaid conditions have been broken for them, and if these Indians are taken out of the protection of the priests mentioned above, no doubt one of two consequences will follow, both in great need of correction and to be feared, because either they will withdraw back into the forest in order to free themselves in that way of their former slavery, with a loss of Faith, theirs and that of the others, or they will resort to arms in defense of their justice and freedom against those who violate their privileges and Your Majesty's laws, avenging themselves on their own behalf since those who have this obligation cannot or do not wish to fulfill it, and in either of these two cases all will be lost.

Your Majesty must take this under consideration and resolve it speedily with the effect that such a great matter demands. What is at risk is the

State, as respect for the Church, the Faith, and the salvation of so many thousands of souls is no less important. May God preserve Your Majesty's powerful person of whom the Christendom and Your Majesty's vassals are so in need.

History of the Future:
The Hopes of Portugal and the
Fifth Empire of the World

CHAPTER ONE

The Presentation here of the first part of the title of this History *and how worthy of human curiosity is its matter.*

Nothing holds more promise for human nature or is more in accord with its greatest appetite or stands above all in this capacity than news of future times and events; and this is what is being offered here to Portugal, Europe, and the World by this new and never before seen history. Other histories tell of past events, this one promises to tell of those yet to come. Others bring back to mind public events that the World has seen; this one intends to show the World those hidden and darkest secrets that have not been penetrated by our understanding. This material soars above the whole sphere of human capacity because God, who is the fountainhead of all wisdom, although He shared his treasures so liberally with mankind (and much more so with the first man), has always kept the knowledge of future things to himself as is the proper prerogative of divinity. Since God, by nature, is eternal, it is the glory of his excellence, not so much for his wisdom as for his eternity, that all future things should be as present for him. Man, the child of time, shares with it his knowledge or his ignorance. He knows little of the present, less of the past, and nothing of the future.

The knowledge of the future, as Plato has said, is what distinguishes the gods from men and out of this there doubtless came to men that ancient appetite to be as gods. For the first men, in whom God had instilled all kinds of knowledge, nothing was lacking except an awareness of future events, and this was promised them by the Devil, along with divinity, when he told them: *Eritis sicut Dii, scientes bonum et malum.*[1] As they experienced his deception, however, they never lost their appetite. This was the heritage that has stayed with us from Paradise. This is the fruit of that fateful tree, forbidden and scantly hungered for but for that very reason more hungered for because it was forbidden.

Since it is the natural inclination of man (and especially since his nature was corrupted) to hunger for what is prohibited and to seek what is denied, his appetite and human curiosity are always knocking at the door of this secret, leaving aside many things that are known, and looking impatiently for a knowledge of things that are to come. In this way the Devil has managed to have man falsely attribute divinity to him, which the Devil, with equal deceit, has also promised to man. And if not, I ask, Who was it that introduced into the World, with no fear whatever, but, rather, with applause, the worship of the Devil? Who made it appear that the idol of Apollo at Delphi be visited and consulted so frequently? Or that of Jupiter in Babylon? Or that of Juno in Carthage? Or that of Venus in Egypt? Or that of Daphne in Antioch? Or that of Orpheus in Lesbos? Or that of Faunus in Italy? Or that of Hercules in Spain? And so many others in so many places? There is no doubt that it was the insatiable desire that men have always had of knowing future things, and the false replies of oracles by which the Devil answers through those statues, that held everything for his worship. It is certain that if God, coming into the World, had not silenced (as he did silence) the oracles of Heathendom, a large part of what today belongs to faith would still be in idolatry. So poorly did men suffer from God's keeping to himself the knowledge of future events that they came to endow stones with the very divinity of God, simply because God had made that knowledge a prerogative of divinity. They would rather have a statue that told them future things than a God who hid these things from them.

But what shall I say of the knowledge or ignorance of the artifacts or superstitions that men have invented, from earth up to heaven, borne along by that appetite? From the four elements they assigned four arts for guessing the future, which took names of their own matter: geomancy, which shows how to prophecy from the look of the land; hydromancy, from that of the water; aeromancy, from that of the air; and pyromancy, from that of fire. So blind were their authors in the vain appetite of that curiosity that, with the vestiges of so many past things having been lost in the land, they think that in water, air, and fire they could discern future events.

In man himself mankind had discovered two always open and manifest books where they could read or spell out this knowledge. Physiognomy, the features of the face; chiromancy, the lines of the hand. In such a small map as the palm of a man's hand the readers not only invented different lines and characteristics but also extrusions that divided and so described the order and succession of life and its events, years, illnesses and dangers, weddings, wars, awards, and all other prosperous or adverse futures. An art that certainly looks true as it puts our future in our hands.

I shall skip over judicial astrology, so famous in the birth of princes, where astrologers, by the basis of one single hour or instant of life, lift up the person or testimonies for all of the events to befall him. Nor do I wish to speak of sad and dismal necromancy, which, frequenting cemeteries and tombs in the darkest and most secret part of night, invokes with pleas and spells the souls of the dead to learn the futures of the living.

To this end they have imagined so many kinds of witchcraft, as if certainty were to be found in the uncertainties of chance. For this end they studied dreams, as though a sleeping man could know more in his sleep than when awake. In this way they consulted the throbbing entrails of animals, as though a dead beast could teach so many living men. With this same appetite they sought answers from springs, rivers, forests, and crags; with this same appetite they queried the songs and flights of birds, the roars of animals, the leaves and movements of trees; with this same appetite they interpreted numbers, names and letters, days, and smoke, shadows and colors, and there was nothing so base or so tiny from which men did not imagine they could grasp that secret which God did not want them to know. The squeak of a door, the shattering of a windowpane, the flicker of a lamp, the stumble of a foot, the shaking of dirt off shoes, everything was taken as a warning from Providence and to be feared as predictions of the future. I speak of the blindness and foolishness of past times so as not to impugn the nobility of our Faith with the superstitions of the present.

Lastly, the investigation of this secret so yearned for has been a study of the arguments of the greatest and most eminent philosophers: Socrates, Pythagoras, Plato, Aristotle, and the eloquent Cicero, in the most sublime and learned books of all their works. There was the famous theology of the Chaldeans, the great mystery of the Egyptians, in Rome the religion of the augurs, in Judea the sect of the Pythians and the Ariolii, in Persia the knowledge and profession of the Magi; finally, all the way from Heaven to Hell, the most fervent zeal of wise men and the greatest longing and blunder of the ignorant, with some insulting Heaven and calling upon the stars to tell them what these cannot and others importuning Hell (as Samuel says), tempting the very demons to reveal what they do not know. So great in all the ages of the World and just as great still today is the appetite of human curiosity, to know the future!

What strengthens the tenacity of this desire more than anything else is the fact that, with mankind so stubbornly deceived by the falsehoods and lies of these arts and their ministers, there has been no experience, nor will there ever be sufficient to open their eyes and draw them away from it: *Genus hominum potentibus infidum, sperantibus fallax, quod in civitate nostra, et vetabitur semper et retinebitur*, says Tacitus.[2] Saul himself, who drove the Sybil away, sought her out and made use of her art. And the very ones who most severely deny any belief in the things predicted, enjoy listening to and knowing what is being predicted, a sure sign that men do not seek future things because they can find them, but that they always pursue them because they love them.

So in order to satisfy the greatest craving of this appetite and ring up the curtain on the greatest and most occult secret of this mystery, today we present this *History* of ours in the theater of the World, and for that reason called *of the Future*. We are not writing with Berosus the ancient histories of the Assyrians, nor with Xenophon those of the Persians, nor with Herodotus those of the Egyptians, nor with Josephus those of the Hebrews, nor with Curtius those of the Macedonians, nor with Thucydides those of the Greeks, nor with Livy those of the Romans, nor with Portuguese writers those of our own. We are writing without an author what none of them wrote or could have written. They wrote histories of the past for future times, we are writing a history of the future for present times. It would seem impossible to paint a copy before there is an original, but this is what the brush of our *History* will do.

In such a way Abel, Isaac, Joseph, and David were portraits of Christ before the Word became man. What the ancient world did not know, what the modern world did not know and what the present cannot grasp is what will be seen, with amazement, in this prodigious map drawn up here: things and events that still lack plenty of time to come into being, much less antiquity.

The earliest history begins with the beginning of the World. The most extensive and continuous ends in the time in which it was written. This history of ours begins in the time in which it is being written, continues all through the duration of the World, and closes with its end. It considers times to come before they come, tells of future happenings before they happen, and describes heroic and famous deeds before fame has made them known and before they have been done.

Time, like the World, has two hemispheres: one above and visible, which is the past, another below and invisible, which is the future. In between these hemispheres are the horizons of time, which are these moments of the present that we are living, where the past ends and the future begins. It is this point from which our *History* takes its start, and it will go along revealing to us the new regions and the new inhabitants of this second hemisphere of time, which is the antipodes of the past. Oh, what great and rare things are to be seen in this new discovery!

The historians we have named, who were the most famous in the World, wrote of empires, republics, laws, councils, resolutions, conquests, battles, victories, the grandeur, the opulence and good fortune, the change, the decline, the ruin of those same nations or others equally powerful with whom they were in contention. We shall also speak of kingdoms and empires, armies and victories, the ruin of some nations and the rise of others, of empires not yet founded, although they shall be founded, of victories not yet won, but that are to be won, of nations not yet mastered and surrendered, but which shall be surrendered and mastered.

To be read in this *History* for the exaltation of the Faith, for the triumph of the Church, for the glory of Christ, for the happiness and universal peace of the World, are high councils, stirring resolutions, religious undertakings, heroic deeds, marvelous victories, amazing conquests, strange and fearsome changes of states, of times, of peoples, of customs, of governments, of laws; but new laws, new governments, new customs, new peoples, new times, new states, new councils and resolutions, new undertakings and deeds, new conquests, victories, peace, triumphs, and good fortune, and not new only because they are future, but because they will have no resemblance to any of those of the past. The World will hear what it has never seen, will read what it has never heard, will admire what it has never read, and will be doubly astounded at what it has never imagined. And if the histories of those writers, being lesser and ancient things of the past, have always been read with pleasure and once known were read again with no boredom, we are confident as we hope that this work of ours will not be displeasing to its readers and that the *History of the Future* will be as delightful to taste and judgment as strange its title and matter are to the paper on which they are written.

However, lest there be some critical curiosity in the fact that the title of *future* does not agree or conform well with the title of *history*, let it be known that it seemed apt to call this writing of ours in this way because, since its plot is new and unheard of, it calls for a name that is new and unheard of too.

Moses wrote the history of the beginning and creation of the World not known until that time by almost all mankind and what was the spirit with which he wrote it? All the Fathers and Doctors answer that it was with the spirit of prophecy. So, then, if in the World there has been a prophet of the past, why should there not be a historian of the future? The prophets did not call their prophecies history because in them they did not follow the style or rules of histories. They did not distinguish among times or point out places. They did not set people apart as individuals, they did not follow the order of cases and events, and when they saw all this and told it all, they wrapped it up in metaphors, disguised it with figures, shaded it with enigmas, and told or sang in phrases that were proper for a prophetic spirit and style, one more based on the majesty and wonderment of mysteries than on their reports and intelligence.

Of the prophet Isaiah, who spoke with greatest order and greatest clarity, Saint Jerome and Saint Augustine said that he wrote more history than prophecy. His prophecy was enclosed in the Gospels and the Gospels are his prophecy revealed. And since we are determined, in everything we write, to observe religiously and pointedly all the rules of history, following along with a clear style that all can understand the order and succession of things, not nakedly and dryly but clothed and accompanied by their circumstances, and because we shall distinguish among times and years, point out provinces and cities, name nations and even people (when the material calls for it), without any ambition or affront to both names, therefore, we call this narration history and *History of the Future*.

Alone and solitary we set out upon it (even more than Noah in the midst of the flood), with neither companion nor guide, neither star nor light, neither exemplary nor example. The sea is immense, the waves are in disorder, the clouds thick, the night deep and dark, but we have hope that the Father of light (whose glory and that of his Son we serve) will bring our fragile little bark to safety with better luck than the Argos and more daring than Typhis.

Before unfurling our sails to the wind (God grant there be no storm), instead of the benevolence that is customarily asked of readers, I want to ask them simply for justice. It is natural law that no one should be condemned without being heard. This is all that is desired and asked of all by this new *History of the Future*, with words that are not its own but from Saint Jerome: *Legant prius et postea despiciant*, "Read first and then condemn." This is what the great master of the Church said in defense of his version of the sacred Books, persecuted and impugned in his time, adored and trusted today.

CHAPTER TWO

Second part of the title of this History: *the Portuguese are invited to hear its lesson.*

In the previous chapter we spoke to the whole World. In this one we speak only to Portugal. In that one we promised grand futures to desire; in this one we offer short desires to the future. Not all futures are to be desired because there are many futures to be feared. "Tomorrow you shall be with me," Samuel said to Saul, the prophet to the king, the dead man to the living one. Oh, what a fearsome future! Saul fell into a faint and it would have been better for him to fall back into his senses than at the feet of the Prophet. But it was already the eve of his death and one who seeks to be undeceived too late is not undeceived. There were other kings who, for not fearing future things, preferred not to know them.

> *Cessant oracular Delphis,*
> *Sed siluit postquam reges timuere futura,*
> *Et Superos vetuere loqui.*[3]

The satirist said without a qualm that kings kept the gods' mouths closed and refused to consult the oracles, for they did not fear future things—whether prosperous or adverse, happy or unhappy. Yet it would have been good to foresee them all, the happy ones for hope and the unhappy for caution.

The greatest service a vassal can render his king is to reveal future things to him, and if there are none among the living who can make these revelations, let them be sought among the buried and they shall be found. Saul found Samuel dead and Balthazar found Daniel alive, because as one killed prophets, the other awarded prophecies. David showed Balthazar the fatal writing on the wall and he announced to him boldly that on that very night Balthazar was to lose his life and his empire. And what did this sad interpretation bring for Daniel? At that same instant—the text says—Balthazar commanded that they dress him in purple and that they give him the royal ring, and that he be recognized by the tristata of the whole empire of the Assyrians, which was a triumvirate or a council of three that exercised the supreme governance of the monarchy.

Balthazar did only this in the instants of life remaining to him, and when the prophet was thus rewarded, the prophecy was fulfilled and the king was dead, deserving only by this act (if his offences had not been sacrilegious) for God to pardon his life.

If knowledge of a future event, even of one so unfortunate, carries so much value; if so much reward is given to a fatal prophecy that brings down empires, what might it have been had empires been promised?

The import of this was not lost on Darius Hidaspes, King of the Persians and the Medes. This victorious prince succeeded to the crown of Balthazar and confirmed Daniel in his good will and the position in which he had been placed, because as he had prophesied that the king of the Assyrians was to lose his empire, he also added that the ruler of the Persians and the Medes was to win it: *Divisum est regnum tuum et datum est Medis et Persis.*[4]

O Portugal (to whom I am only speaking now), I expect neither your thanks nor do I fear your ingratitude. Because if you do not count with Daniel among the living, I count myself with Samuel among the dead; if in the letters that I interpret I had found misfortunes (it is quite possible that you will have them), I would have told you about bad luck with no misgivings, just as I shall tell you the good with no adulation. But such is your star (God's blessing must be upon you) that everything I read about you is greatness, everything I discover is betterment, everything I grasp is good fortune. This is what you must expect and this is what is in expectation of you. Therefore, as a subtitle and a more definite one, I call this same writing the *Hopes of Portugal*, and this is a brief summation of all the *History of the Future*.

I see, however, that the very name *Hopes of Portugal* can, with good reason, hold back pleasure, frighten desire, and hinder the very enthusiasms I have placed before you with these hopes. *Spes quae differtur, affligit animam*, the divine Truth has said, and human experience and patience know it and feel it quite well.[5] Even though hope might be quite secure, quite firm, and quite well founded, awaiting its fruit is a hopeless torment.

Most certain and as certain as is the very word of God (who cannot lie or be wrong) were the promises of the ancient Prophets, but desire wearied so much in the patient awaiting for them to come true that the hopes of the prophecies became a fable of the masses in Jerusalem. Isaiah speaks of this complaint in Chapter 28, saying that in the streets and on the squares of the city people went about singing with laughter at their hopes and that the chorus or refrain was:

Expecta, reexpecta,
Expecta, reexpecta,
Modicum ibi,
Modicum ibi.[6]

Those men hoped, hoped again, and lost hope because in many of the things promised them by the prophecies, life ended before the hope arrived. Fathers handed down the hopes in their wills to their sons, sons to their grandsons, and not even those, although lives were longer then, got to see the fulfillment of what they had hoped for so long. Abraham left the hopes for the Promised Land to Isaac, Isaac to Jacob, and Jacob to the twelve Patriarchs, but they all died and were buried in Egypt. What can the Promised Land mean to them who are to be covered by Egyptian earth? In captivity in Babylon the Prophets preached and promised that God would lift his hand of punishment and restore the people to their former freedom. And if they were asked when, they would reply and affirm always seventy years from then.

Some hope it was for a captive, even if he was not too old! What use is the hope of freedom for me if my life is to end first? The same can be argued by those who are living today about these hopes that I promise them. Great are these hopes for Portugal, but when is Portugal to see them?

This is a point that will be dealt with very pointedly later on and which in our *History* will take up all of the fifth book. For now I can only say that I would not dare promise hopes if they were not short hopes. God in his Written Law, as great authors have noted, never expressly promised Heaven because what cannot be given immediately is not to be promised. To promise Heaven and go along waiting for it in Limbo is a promise that gives the contrary of what is promised. Such are postponed hopes. If they promise life, they are death; if Paradise is promised, they are Hell.

Limbo was called Hell. Why? Because it was a place where Paradise was hoped for over so many years. Do not let my Homeland consider me so cruel as to promise it martyrdom in the name of hope. For hope to be worthwhile the future must be measured.

Saint Paul, that philosopher of the third Heaven, challenging all creatures and their times, divided the future into two futures: *Neque instantia, neque futura.*[7] A future that is distant and another that is near, a future that for a long time will be future—*neque futura*—and another future that shortly will be present: *Neque instantia.*

This second future is the one of my *History*, and these are the brief and delightful hopes that I offer Portugal. Hopes that will be read by those who see, and that will be seen by those who live, even though they may not live for many years, but those who see them will live many years. *Lignum vitae, desiderium veniens*, as was said above in the same place, professing the same divine Truth.[8]

Thus, just as there are hopes that take a long time, there are hopes that come. The hopes that come are the fruit of the tree of life: *Lignum vitae desiderium veniens*. The miraculous quality of that fruit was to improve and lengthen life and restore youth to those who ate it.

The hopes that delay take away life. The hopes that come not only do not take away life but they lengthen its days and breath: *Spes quae differtur, affligit animam; lignum vitae, desiderium veniens*.

What life will there be in Portugal so weary, what age so decrepit, that at the sight of the fulfillment of these hopes it will not turn back the years to attain so much good? Live, live, you Portuguese, you who merited to live in this fortunate century! Have hope in the Author of such strange promises, because the one who gave you these hopes will show you their fulfillment.

This is not a privilege of just any prophecy, but of those prophecies of which this *History* is composed. Yes, because they are more than prophecies. One prophet there was in the World who was more than a prophet, who was the great precursor of Christ. And why did Saint John, among all the prophets in this World, bear the singularity of this name? Because the other prophets promised a future Christ, but did not see him or show him to be present. The Baptist promised the future Christ with his voice and pointed out the present Christ with his finger—*Cecinit ad futurum, et adesse monstravit*.

If there was a prophet who was more than a prophet, why are there not also some prophecies that are more than prophecies? Thus I hope will be the ones on which my hopes are based and which, if they promise future good fortune, will also show a present one. Now they promise with their voice, later they will point them out with their finger.

But let this great matter await its proper place. I can only say that when it happens that way, this *History* of ours will gloriously lose its name and will cease to be the *History of the Future*, for it will be that of the present.

Yet some foreign rival may ask me (because I do not answer the native ones): if the expected Empire, as your title itself claims, is of the World, why are the hopes also not of the World rather than just of Portugal? The reason (with apologies to that same World) is this: because the best part of the fortunate future events that are expected, and the most glorious of them, will not only belong to the Portuguese Nation, but uniquely and singularly be its own. Portugal will be the substance, Portugal the center, Portugal the theater, Portugal the beginning and the end of these wonders, and the prodigious instruments of them will be the Portuguese.

See now, oh my Homeland, how agreeable it shall be for you, and with how much pleasure you should accept the offer that I make you with this new *History*, and with what enthusiasm, pleasure and joy your reason and natural love ask you to read it and to consider its future and your future. The Greek reads with greatest pleasure the histories of Greece, the Roman those of Rome, and the Barbarian those of his nation, because they are reading deeds of theirs and of their forebears. And Portugal, who with a novelty unheard of will read in this *History* its own and those of its descendants, with how much greater pleasure and contentment, with how much greater applause and enthusiasm will have the reason to do so?

Amazing were those deeds in the past, oh Portuguese, those with which you discovered new seas and new lands, and from these led the World to know the very World itself. Thus, as you then read those histories of yours, read now this one of mine, which is also all yours. You revealed to the World what it was, and I shall reveal to you what you are to be. In no way is this discovery of mine subordinate or lesser, but greater in all ways. A greater Gama, a greater Cape, a greater Hope, a greater Empire.

In those happy times (less happy, however, than future ones) nothing was read about in the World except the voyages and conquests of the Portuguese. This History will put all histories to silence. Enemies will read their ruination in it, imitators their envy, and only Portugal its glory. Such is the *History*, Portuguese, that I present to you, and, therefore, in your language. If the World is to be restored to its primitive wholeness and natural beauty, such a great body cannot be put together without pain or feeling in its members, which are out of joint. Some moans will be heard amidst your cheers, but these too make for harmony if they are from enemies. For the enemies there will be pain, for imitators envy, for friends and companions pleasure, and for you, finally, glory, and in the meantime Hopes.

CHAPTER THREE
Third part of the title and division of the whole History.

What the third part of the title of this History contains can only be put forth completely by the discourse of it all, because all of it is employed in proving the hope of a new Empire, which for reasons to be seen in due time, we shall call the Fifth. However, just so the material will be understood right away and the reader will know quickly what we are promising him, I shall lay out a brief description of its division.

The *History of the Future* is divided into seven parts or books: in the first it will be shown that there is to be a new Empire in the World; in the second what Empire this is to be; in the third its great deeds and good fortunes; in the fourth, the means by which it is to be brought about; in the fifth in what land; in the sixth at what time; in the seventh in what person. These seven things are the ones that the new History we are writing about the Fifth Empire of the World will examine, resolve, and prove.

But since the word World, in the ambitious titles of Empires and Emperors, is accustomed to have greater thunder in its sound than truth in its meaning, it would be well for us to say right here what the title of our *History* means by World.

The Pharaohs of Egypt and also the Ptolemies who succeeded them in such a way measured the narrowness of their land with the arrogance and vanity of their vast thoughts, that while dominating only that no so large part of the edge of Africa, lying between the deserts of Numidia and those of the Red Sea, they did not hesitate to give themselves the title of Lords of the World. That was the disparity of the name that the Egyptians gave to their restorer, Joseph: *Vocaverunt eum lingua aegyptiaca Salvatorem Mundi.*[10] They did not call him Savior of Egypt, but of the World, as though there were not other world but Egypt. They were imitating the haughtiness of their haughty Nile, which, when it reaches the sea, spreads out into seven mouths, as though there were seven rivers, it being just one river. This was the way of that Empire and others called "of the World," greater always in name than in body and vastness.

Of the Empire of the Assyrians we have in divine letters a writ mentioned in Prophet Daniel's three chapters and ordered by the great Nebuchadnezzar, the introduction of which is as follows: *Nabuchodonosor, rex omnibus populis, gentibus et linguis, qui habitant in universa terra*; Nebuchadnezzar, king of all peoples, nations, and languages that dwell in the whole World.[11] And what is more, Daniel himself speaking to this king and following the customs of his court and the magnificent titles of his greatness, calls him thus in the same chapter: *Tu ... rex ... magnificatus es et invaluisti, et magnitudo tua ... pervenit usque ad caelum, et potestas tua in terminos universae terrae.*[12] However if we lay out the limits of the

THE SERMON OF SAINT ANTHONY TO THE FISH AND OTHER TEXTS

lands that obeyed Nebuchadnezzar, we would find that of the Asia known at that time he had a goodly part, of Africa little, of Europe less, and of the rest of the World nothing. But these three slices of land were enough for the arrogance of Nebuchadnezzar to endow the titles of his empire with the thunderous one of all the World. So great was the meaning of the names and so little what they stood for!

Of the Empire of Xerxes (which was that of the Persians) the Sacred Text says in the first chapter of the story of Esther that it extended from India to Ethiopia, with 127 provinces showing obedience to that crown. This was the demarcation of the lands and these the borders of the Empire, but the titles had no limits. Thus it is told us in a decree of Darius's, which is referred to in Chapter Six of Daniel, in these pompous words, similar in all respects to those of Nebuchadnezzar: *Darius rex … omnibus populis et gentibus et linguis, qui habitant in universa terra: Pax vobis multiplicetur.*[13] And Xerxes himself in another decree, in Chapter Thirteen of Esther, signed in his own hand that he had subject to his domain the whole world: *Cum … universum orbem meae ditioni subjugassem.*[14] So the Persian kings, by being lords of 127 provinces, passed provisos and decrees to the whole World, but anyone who unrolled the map of the World and laid on it the parchments of these decrees would easily see that the World is, without too much exaggeration, one hundred and twenty-seven times larger than the Persian Empire. How little does the geography of the titles match the measure of the Empires!

What shall I say of the Empire of the Romans? The boundaries that its writers point out are the limits of the World:

> *Orbem jam totum victor Romanus habebat.*
> *Qua mare, qua terra, qua sidus currit utrumque.*[15]

Petronius said, and Cicero, who professed more truth than the poets: *Nulla gens est, quae non aut ita sublata sit, ut vix exstet, aut ita domita, ut quiescat, aut ita pacata, ut victoria nostra imperioque laetetur.*[16] Such was the opinion that Rome had of its greatness and such is the style that it followed in its edicts: *exiit edictum a Caesare Augusto* (says Saint Luke) *ut describeretur universus orbis.*[17]

Caesar Augustus ordered his Empire to be registered and listed, and the edict said: Let the World be listed! But if we examine this Roman world up to where it reached, we would find that in the east it stopped at the Tigris, in the west at the sea of Cadiz, in the south at the Nile, and in the north at the Danube and the Rhine. These limits were established by Claudian, although he gave the eastern borders:

> subdidit Oceanum sceptris et margine caeli
> clausit opes, quantum distant a Tigride Gades,
> inter se Tanais quantum Nilusque relinquunt.[18]

I leave out the Mongol, the Chinese, the Tartar, the Turk, and other barbarian domains of our time, which with the same majesty of titles call themselves Emperors of the World, following the ancient arrogance of Asia, where the World was always attached to titles of monarchy.

The world of our promised Empire is not the World in this sense. I do not promise worlds, or titular empires, names as lacking in modesty as in truth. I know quite well that the Empire of Germany (the aged and almost finished relic of the Roman) is in many texts, by one or another right, called Empire of the World. But it is also known that texts can give titles, but not empires. In the seventh book we shall examine the bases of this right. However, even though we grant it liberally, it is certain that empires and kingdoms are not defended by the sword of justice but by the justice of the sword.

God promised Abraham the lands of Palestine, but they were conquered by the sword of Joshua and defended by that of his successors. These are the human instruments which serve (even though working divinely) the Providence of that supreme Lord, who is the Lord of the World and of Armies. Those who wish the noise to fill in some way the emptiness of these great titles say that they are understood to be hyperbole or exaggeration, or that figure of speech that rhetoricians call synecdoche, in which the part stands for the whole. The title of this *History* does not speak through hyperboles or synecdoches, it does not call a pygmy gigantic, nor an arm a man. The World of which I speak is the World, that World, and in that meaning with which Saint John said, *Mundus per ipsum factus est, et Mundus cum non cognovit.*[19] The World that God created, the World that did not know him, and the World that is to know him. When it did not know him, it denied him dominion. When it knows him, it will give him possession: *universum terrarum orbem*—says Ortelius—*veteres ... in tres partes divisere: Africam, Europam et Asiam, sed inventa America, eam pro quarta parte nostra aetas adjecit; quintamque expectat sub meridionali cardine jacentem.* "The World that the Ancients knew was divided into three parts: Africa, Europe, Asia; after America was discovered, our age added this fourth part to it. The fifth part is now awaited, which is that unknown but already recognized land that we call Austral."[20]

This was the past World, this is the present World, and this will be the future World; and these three worlds together will make up (for God shapes it this way) a whole World. This is the subject of our *History*, and this is the empire we promise the World. Everything that the sea embraces, everything that the Sun's light illuminates, everything that the sky covers and encircles will be subject to this Fifth Empire, not by a fantastic name or title like all those that up till now have called themselves Empires of the World, but through true domination and rule. All kingdoms will be united under one scepter, all heads will obey one supreme head, all crowns will end in one single diadem, and this will be the pedestal of the Cross of Christ.

Augustus resolved with the senate to place limits on the vastness of the Roman Empire. Tacitus had doubts as to whether this resolution was the child of apprehension or envy: *Incertum metu, an per invidiam.*[21] Caesar feared (if it was apprehension) that such an enormously huge body could not be animated with a single spirit, could not be governed by a single head, could not be defended by a single arm; or he did not want (if it was envy) to be succeeded by another more successful Emperor who would go beyond the boundaries of what he had conquered up till then and might be or be called greater than Augustus. This was, they say, the thought of Alexander, who, when close to death, divided his empire among different successors so that none could inherit his name of Great. It is not nor can it be thus in the Empire of the World that we promise. Peace will remove apprehension, union will undo envy, and God (who is unchanging good fortune) will maintain its greatness.

Here ends the title of this *History*, and in a clearer way than what we are saying now we shall prove it later on. In the meantime, however, if insistence comes to the learned and doubt to the scrupulous, let us make use of the divine hand as a solution to all of these: *sciant et recogitent, et intelligant … quia manus Domini fecit hoc.*[22]

CHAPTER FOUR
The Uses of the History of the Future

If the aim of this writing were only the satisfaction of human curiosity and the pleasure or flattery of that appetite with which the impatience of our desire moves forward as it wants to know of future things, and if the hopes that we have promised were only flowers with no other fruit than the enthusiasm and joy with which one's own great and good fortunes are accustomed to be expected, I most certainly would stop my pen immediately and throw it away, considering this effort of mine to be useless, impertinent, and idle, and to be unworthy not only of being communicated to the World, but a waste of time and care.

But if the history of past things (which wise men called the schoolmistress of life) has this and so many other uses necessary for the government and common good of humankind and for the particular affairs of all men, and if this being the case so many illustrious minds employed their superior knowledge, skill and judgment in its cultivation, immortalizing their memory with their writings throughout the ages, why should not this *History of the Future* of ours be equally useful and profitable, or indeed even more so, since men's spirits are moved more powerfully and effectively with the hope of their own affairs than with the memory of those of others?

If we count in all the sacred Books the writers of past things (who were the four Evangelists in the Law of Grace and in Scripture Moses, Joshua, Samuel, Esdras, and some few others whose names are not known with such proven certainty), we will find that there is a much greater number of those who wrote of future things: a difference that God, who is the real Author of all Scripture (all of it having been written, as Saint Paul says, for our instruction) would surely not have made, if the use that we can and should derive from a knowledge of future events were not greater than news of those of the past. And, truly, if the benefits of knowledge are gained and known better through the evils of ignorance, one who meditates on events in the World from its beginning to the present will easily find that these were fewer harms that befell men for a lack of knowledge of the past than those into which they rushed blindly for an ignorance of the future.

As a consequence of this truth and in consideration of the things that I have set about to write, I say, Christian reader, that all those purposes we know Divine Providence had at diverse times, in different places and nations, to reveal in anticipation things that were still to come, flow together in particular harmony toward this our *History* and in it are joined. And this is not just the main reason, but the singular and total one, for which we have subjected ourselves to the work of such a burdensome form of writing, hoping that it will be pleasing to and accepted by God, whom we are only attempting to serve, understanding that it was the will, inspiration, and even the gentle force of Providence itself that gave the impulses that brought us (not without some struggle) to this task, so that these secrets of its hidden judgment and counsel might be uncovered and brought to light for the World and through it all bring about in due proportion the effects of change, betterment, and reform to which they are aimed and directed. To the divine Majesty himself, humbly prostrating ourselves before his infinite reverence, we ask with all the affection of our heart, now that we are reaching the major import of this material, that he be inclined to lend us that light, grace, and spirit needed for such an arduous task, knowing and confessing that without the presence of this sovereign assistance neither will we know how to explain to others the little which through Heaven's mercy we have reached and known, nor even less will we be able to reveal and attain in seeking out so much that remains to be known.

THE FIRST USE

The first and principal reason for why God has been accustomed to reveal future things (whether benefits or punishments) a long time before they happen is so men will know, clearly and firmly, that they all come dispensed by his hand. Eternal Wisdom arms itself in this way against human nature, which is always prideful, rebellious, and ungrateful, either in order that it should not swell its pride with the divine benefits, and kiss its own hands, as Job said, or so that it should not attribute to the natural order of things (and much less to chance) the effects that come handed down as punishment by its Justice or ordained for higher and hidden ends by its Providence. Shown to Pharaoh in dreams were the seven seeded stalks and the seven unseeded ones, the seven thin cows and the seven fat ones, and Divine Providence immediately arranged for there to appear in Egypt a Joseph (even though sold into slavery and exiled), who would clarify the mystery of the seven lush years and the seven hungry ones, so that the barbarian would know that God and not his worshiped Nile was the author of both abundance and want, and that he should be thankful for the benefit of the seven years and the remedy for all fourteen. Since it never rains in the land of Egypt and fields are irrigated and fertilized by floods from the River Nile, Pliny said wisely that only the Egyptians did not look to Heaven because they did not expect sustenance from there as did other nations.

Oh, how many Christians are there, like Egyptians, who neither expecting nor fearing lift their eyes to Heaven and instead of revering in all things the first cause only worship the second ones! That was why God showed Pharaoh so many years back what were to be the years of famine and those of plenty, so that the ignorant wisdom of Egypt would know the means of the conservation or ruin of kingdoms were handed down by the omnipotent hand of God when they come about, for only He can determine beforehand for them to be.

The same Providence, as we have said above, wished to take away the Empire of Belshazzar and give it to Darius, but first there appeared the sentence written in the palace of Babylon and there was a Daniel (also a captive and an exile) to interpret the mysteries of it for the king, so that Belshazzar, who was losing his throne, should know that he was losing it because God was taking it away from him; and so that Darius, who was to receive it, should understand that he was receiving it because God was giving it to him. God is the one who gives and takes away kingdoms and empires, when and to whom it pleases him. And of no use, if God decides otherwise, are either Darius's arms to gain it or Belshazzar's right of inheritance to keep it. For this reason wishes Divine Providence for these sentences to be written before they are carried out and that there be someone to interpret them before it happens.

The wondrous future events of the World and of Portugal, with which our *History* is to deal, were dreamed many years ago like those of Pharaoh and written down like those of Belshazzar, but up till now there has been no Joseph to interpret the dreams nor any Daniel to construe the writings. And this is what I am setting out to do, with the grace of that Lord who is always served by small instruments for great matters, so that the World and Portugal should know, with their eyes always upon Heaven and upon God, that all of it is the result of his power and the counsel of his Providence. And so that there be no ignorance so blind nor ambition so haughty that it takes away from God what is of God to give to Caesar what is not of Caesar, attributing to luck or human industry what must only be from divine disposition.

This was the manner with which God has always dealt with Portugal, wary, perhaps, of a nation that is so much the friend of honor and glory that it might want to steal his. Anyone looking at Portugal in past times, the present, and the future, will see it born in the past, revived in the present, and glorious in the future. In all three differences in times and styles, God revealed to it and deemed it first to interpret the outstanding favors and mercies with which he decided to ennoble it: in the first by making it, in the second by restoring it, and in the third by glorifying it.

Before the birth of Portugal, Christ himself appeared to the not yet King Dom Afonso Henriques and revealed to him that it was his wish to make him king and Portugal a kingdom, the victory that he was to give him in such dubious battle and the arms of such glory with which he wanted to make it stand out among all the kingdoms of the World. And the ambassador and interpreter of this and other futures which would later be fulfilled was that old man, unknown and withdrawn from the world, the hermit of the field of Ourique, so that Portugal would know and could not deny that it owed to God the victory and the crown, and that it was all his from the moments of its birth.

Before Portugal's resurrection, which we all also saw, the event and all its circumstances were revealed, and there was no one who did not know or who had not read that in the year forty there would rise up in Portugal a new king and that his name would be John. And the interpreter of this future which seemed so impossible, and of so many others that were later fulfilled and are being fulfilled, was another humble individual, also withdrawn from the world although very well known among us: that craftsman from Trancoso who, not knowing how to read or write, made up prodigious accounts of these wonders, in order that Portugal would know again that it is to God and to no other that the restitution of the crown was owed, which sixty years before had fallen or been torn from its head.

Before the glories of Portugal, which is the future time, and many hundreds and even thousands of years before (as we shall show), this third and most fortunate state of our Kingdom has also been revealed and along with it the miraculous means and instruments through which it is to rise and be lifted up to the highest and most sublime of all human happiness. And the interpreter of this last and most glorious state of Portugal is who I have already said and how unworthy he is for it, and for that reason very much in keeping (as befits God's style) for such a grand and difficult enterprise, so that even with this circumstance the Portuguese will know that the same omnipotent hand that for twenty-four years has conserved and defended so faithfully and victoriously the Kingdom of Portugal is the one that is to raise it up and glorify it (perchance in a much smaller number of years) to the most fortunate and glorious state that it has been promised.

Let the Portuguese consider now and read all that we shall be writing and laying before them with this premise and most important warning: that if something were to hold back the fulfillment of these promises from them, it could only be their forgetting or not knowing the sovereign Author of them, when to our misfortune we could be so insultingly ungrateful to God that we ascribed the past benefits or hopes for the future ones to a hand other than this.

God promised to free the children of Israel from captivity in Egypt, as he had sworn to their elders, and to lift them up and give them possession of the Promised Land. And although all saw the fulfillment of the first promise, miraculously obtaining their freedom and shaking off without bloodshed or the sword the subjection to such a powerful domain, being, all told, more than six hundred thousand men who triumphed over Pharaoh and crossed over to the other bank of the Red Sea, of all of them none entered the Promised Land or succeeded in gaining the good fortune and rest of the second promise except Joshua and Caleb, two of those twelve adventurers who, chosen by the Twelve Tribes, went on ahead to explore the land. A rare example of severity in God's mercy, but a well-deserved punishment; because if we search the Holy Text for the causes of this deviation and delay (which lasted forty whole years, while the distance of the road was short and might have been covered in a few days), we will find that they were three. We shall now make use of two, then we will speak of the third.

The first cause was the attribution of the freedom from captivity to Moses, as was said in Chapter Thirty-Two of the Exodus: *Moysi enim huic viro, qui nos eduxit de terra Aegypti, ignoramus quid acciderit.*[23] The second, and even more ignorant (as well as impious and blasphemous), was their attributing that same freedom to the idol that they had constructed in the desert from their gold and impiously prayed to it in loud voices: *Hi sunt dii tui, Israel, qui te eduxerunt de terra Aegypti.*[24]

Enough, discourteous, ungrateful, and blasphemous people! Were Moses and your idol those who freed you from captivitiy in Egypt? God certainly did not say this to Moses himself when he gave him his office and his staff and made him, against so much repugnance, the instrument of his powers: *Vidi adflictionem populi mei in Aegypto et clamorem eius audivi; et sciens dolorem eius, descendi ut liberarem eum de manibus Aegyptiorum et educerem de terra illa in terram bonam et spatiosam in terram quae fluit lacte et melle.*[25] "I saw," God says, "the affliction of my people and I heard their cries; and because I know how just are their complaints, I descended in person to free them from the hands of the Egyptians and take them out of that land for another, which I am to give them good, spacious, abundant and full of pleasures and delights." So that the one who brought the children of Israel out of Egypt was God, and the one who opened the Red Sea and drowned Pharaoh and his armies in it was God, and the one who made the miracles and wonders was God. And those who attribute the works of God and the rewards (for which only he is owed thanks) to Moses and to the idol do not deserve to have life or eyes to seek out and see the Promised Land. It was very just and justified punishment that all should die and end before reaching the time set for good fortune, and that, since they had interpreted the gift of the first promise so ungratefully and so impiously, they be deprived of the enjoyment of the second.

I do not deny that with any good sense Moses can be called the liberator from captivity or that God also gave him that name to honor him; but for the men who should have given God all the glory (because it was all his), referring it to Moses was a discourtesy, attributing it to the idol was blasphemy, and not giving it all to God was the greatest ingratitude.

Now God, oh, Portuguese, has freed us from captivity; now, through God's mercy, we have triumphed over Pharaoh and the power of his armies; now we have seen them, not once, but many times drowned in the Red Sea of their own blood. We have gone walking through the desert toward the Promised Land and it may be that we are already quite near to it and to the ultimate fulfillment of the promised bounties. If there is someone so envious of the blessings of the Homeland and such an enemy of himself that he wishes to delay the course of such a prosperous and happy journey and end his life unhappily before seeing the desired end of it, let him deny God what is God's and attribute freedom, victories, and the fulfillment of the first promises that we have seen, either to Moses or to the idol. Whoever refers the glories of good events to the prince, to the general, to the minister, is giving God's glory to Moses; whoever refers the glories of good events to his valor, to his military knowledge, to his arm, to his talent, is giving God's glory to the idol. Therefore here are written for you this same freedom, those same victories, and those same events, the ones that have been seen and the ones that remain to be seen, so many years ago revealed by God. That the whole World may know by our confession that they are acts of his commiseration and not the work of our power; and that we, as the effects of divine Providence, Goodness, and Omnipotence, may refer them only to God, and praise only God and give thanks to him.

The enemies I most fear for Portugal are pride and ingratitude, vices so natural to good fortune that, like children of the viper, they at once are born from it and corrupt it. Humility and thankfulness, mistrust of ourselves and trust in God, and the zeal and the purest desire for his glory, yielding to it him in everything and for everything, are always the sure means that are to sustain us, lift us up, and put us in possession of these second promises. And this knowledge, so pleasing to God, which we learn in the notice of his future things, is the first fruitful use that can be drawn from the lesson of this our *History*, as important for life as for our sight.

A BRIEF WARNING FOR THE INCREDULOUS

But before we pass on to the other uses, which will remain for the subsequent chapters, it will be proper for us to close this one with the third cause of the punishment that we have been pondering, to which the Sacred Text refers in Chapter Fourteen of Numbers and which can serve as a great example for another caste of people, those whom Scripture calls *children of little faith.*

With the arrival of the twelve explorers of the Promised Land, all agreed on the width, goodness, and fertility of the land; but except for Joshua and Caleb, who facilitated the conquest and encouraged the people to it, the others all stated, on the contrary, that it was impossible, as much because of the fortification and location of the cities as for the valor, strength, and size of the men, who, compared to the Hebrews (they said), looked like giants. In the end numbers prevailed over reason (as happens so many times). The people determined to elect a captain and to return with him to captivity in Egypt, the experience of so many past victories and so many unheard of events and miracles, and, above all, the divine promises so repeatedly implanted that God was to give them possession of that land not having been enough for them to believe and trust that it was to be that way.

This cowardly belief was the last lack of reason to finally scoff at divine patience. And God, having resolved not to endure such people anymore, nor to pardon them or dissemble, as he had done up to then, decided for there to be brought down upon them the sentence of their own disbelief; and since they believed that God was not going to give them possession of the Promised Land, none of them should enter into nor see it, and all would die first and be buried in that desert. Thus he spoke and thus it was brought to pass.

God's words of complaint and of his sentence were these: *Usquequo detrahet mihi populus iste? Quousque non credent mihi in omnibus signis, quae feci coram eis? ... Vivo ego, ait Dominus, sicut locuti estis, audiente me, sic faciam vobis. In solitudine hac jacebunt cadavera vestra; ... non intrabitis terram, super quam levavi manum meam, ut habitare vos facerem.*[26]

Let disbelievers and the spiritless (both vices I do not know whether from little or evil hearts) read and weigh well these words of God and let them see the danger into which their disbelief can place them or has placed them: *Sicut locuti estis, sic faciam vobis.*[27] Those who from the experience of what they have seen believe what is promised will see it, because they are worthy of seeing it; for those who do not believe, or do not wish to believe, their very disbelief will be their punishment, and since they did not believe it, they will not see it. Saint Augustine (whose excellent words we shall quote further on) says that after a part of the promises are fulfilled, not believing that the others are to be fulfilled is not only an obstinacy of rational disbelief, but a sin of great ingratitude against the divine Author of the rewards themselves. And his Providence punishes these disbelievers and ingrates most justly by not letting them see or enjoy what they do not wish to believe of its goodness: *Quousque non credent mihi in omnibus signis quae feci coram eis?*

Before the experience of the first miracles, some excuse could be made for disbelief in the weakness of human fear and mistrust, but after so many, so great, so wonderful, and so strange things having been fulfilled and seen by eyes, to disbelieve still in those that are to come is a rebellion of ingratitude and a hardness of distrust, both deserving of God's punishment by conforming to them: *Sicut locuit estis, sic faciam vobis.*

Whoever wishes to know (according to the usual manner of divine Justice and Providence) if he is to come to see the good fortune that we promise him here under this word, let him examine his heart and consult his faith; from our own heart God cuts out our sentence and from our own words its form: *Ex ore tuo te judico.*[28] To those who believe, like the Centurion, Christ says: *Sicut credidisti, fiat tibi.*[29] And to those who do not believe, like the Israelites in the desert, God says: *Sicut locuti estis, sic faciam vobis.* For him who believes that those so happy promises will be fulfilled, it will be thus, and he shall see them and enjoy them: *Sicut credidisti, fiat tibi.* And to him who does not believe they are to be fulfilled, it will also be thus: he shall not enjoy them or see them. It is the law of God's generosity to pay faith with sight and therefore we are to see in Heaven the mysteries in which we believe on Earth. And this way that God is accustomed to use in the glory of the other life he also uses ordinarily in the bounties of this one, when he has promised them: those who believe in them shall have life to see them; those who do not believe in them shall die, so that they shall not see them. Thus has God himself ordered once again in a similar case through the mouth of the prophet Habakkuk: *Ecce qui incredulus est, non erit recta anima ejus in semetipso, justus autem in fide sua vivet.*[30] "The disbeliever," God says, "will not have a secure life; and to the one who believes, his faith itself will conserve life." This is how it happened, because in the war that Nebuchadnezzar waged against Jerusalem, those who believed the prophets lived, along with King Jechonias, and those who did not wish to believe perished with King Sedecias. He who does not believe is not worthy of the sight, and in order that he should not see God takes his life away. Let the disbelievers look for themselves, and if they do not believe that we are to see, let them believe that they are not to live: *Si non credieritis, non permanebitis*, says the prophet Isaiah.[31]

CHAPTER FIVE
Second Use

The second use of this *History*, more needed by nearby and present times, is the patience, constancy, and consolation during the difficulties, dangers, and calamities with which the world is to be afflicted and purified before the awaited good fortune arrives.

When the farmer wishes to plant again where there is wild growth, first he takes his ax, cuts, fells, burns, uproots, clears, digs, and then plants and sows. When the architect wishes to build again over old ruins, he also begins by tearing down, undoing, clearing, and uprooting all the way down to the foundations, and then, on his new base, he works a new plan and raises a new building. This is what the Supreme Creator and Craftsman of the World does and has done when he wishes to plant and build again. This is what he said and has ordered the whole World to be notified of through the prophet Jeremiah: *Ecce constitui te hodie super gentes et super regna, ut evellas, et destruas, et disperdas, et dissipes, et aedifices, et plantes.*[32]

Oh peoples, kings, and kingdoms! How much uprooting, how much destruction, how much loss, how much dissipation will be seen in your lands, fields, and cities before God replants and rebuilds you and the Universe is seen to be restored and renewed! It is a miracle that was promised many years ago for this last age of the World by that supreme Monarch who sits on his throne over it all: *Et dixit qui sedebat in throno: Ecce nova facio omnia.*[33] And so that no one should doubt such a new and unusual thing, the Evangelical Prophet adds immediately after: *Haec verba fidelissima sunt et vera.*[34]

If some part of these difficulties and punishments should fit Portugal, and if it is one of the kingdoms of Christendom that deserves to be all renovated and reformed, let Portugal itself examine and, if it knows itself, let it judge, reminding itself that it has been written that the judgment and example of God are to begin in his house: *Judicium incipiet a domo Dei.*[35] But be it for Portugal or for the rest of the World, or for all people (as is most certain), mankind will have nothing of greater consolation, relief, or remedy for the suffering and constant endurance of such strong calamities than the lesson and contemplation of this *History of the Future*, not for what it says of ours, but for the original Scriptures from which it has been drawn. This is their aim, Saint Paul says, and the principal fruit of their writing: *Quaecumque scripta sunt, ad nostram doctrinam scripta sunt, ut per patientiam et consolationem scripta sunt, ut per patientiam et consolationem Scriptorum spem habeamus.*[36]

The lesson of the Scriptures, and the knowledge of and faith in future things, is what more than anything else can console us in hardships, because patience has its consolation in hope, hope has its basis in faith, and faith is based on the Scriptures.

What greater hardship or peril can befall a republic than to see itself surrounded and set upon on all sides by powerful enemies, alone and unprotected, and without friend or ally who can help it? This was the state in which the Maccabees saw themselves so many times during their rule, a state from which God always freed them with miraculous victories and heavenly aid, so that it was not necessary for them to make use of the confederation they had at that time with the Romans and the Spartans, and the Spartans themselves were informed of this by Jonathan, who governed the people then, saying in a letter: *Nos cum nullo horum indigeremus, habentes solatio sanctos libros, qui sunt in manibus nostris, maluimus mittere ad vos renovare fraternitatem et amicitiam.*[37] We order restored through this our ambassador (Jonathan says) the old friendship and confederation that our elders had made with you, not because we have need of it and of your help, although we do not lack for enemies, wars, oppressions, and hardships; but because we always have in our hands the Holy Books in which we read the divine promises, and with the Books and the promises we console ourselves and take heart to resist, fight, and prevail as we have prevailed and shall prevail over all our enemies.

In Chapter Eight it will be seen that with no insolence or too great confidence we can call this *History of the Future* of ours a holy book. If there are to be (as there must be first) hardships, perils, oppressions, tribulations, wars, battles, deaths, bloodshed, destruction, devastations, and all manner of calamities, miseries, and lashings by which God is accustomed to punish, correct, and tame the rebellion of human hearts, for such most trying occasion this holy book is divulged and given to the World and in it the afflicted will find relief, the downhearted consolation, the troubled remedy, the assaulted assistance, the doubting hope, patience, constancy, and strength, all by means of the lesson and faith of the divine promises and the contemplation of the most felicitous purposes for which all these troubles and tribulations have been ordered by the Supreme Providence.

It is quite worthy of note that never among the people of Israel had so many Prophets come together as before the Babylonian captivity and in that same captivity. Before the captivity those prophesying were, in order, Hosea, Isaiah, Joel, and Amos; during the captivity those prophesying were Micah, Habakkuk, Jeremiah, Ezekiel, Daniel, and Zephaniah. So that, there being only sixteen canonical Prophets, ten of them had for the main matter of all their prophecies the Babylonian captivity. The first four, who wrote more than a hundred years before that time, prophesied that the people would be made captives for their sins, but through God's mercy would later be restored to their homeland. The other six, who prophesied during the time of captivity, repeated constantly that it was to have an end, pointedly determining the year of their freedom.

The reason behind such an extraordinary agreement of Prophets and prophecies (never before or after seen) was that never before had the people of Judah seen such a great difficulty and calamity as the captivity and the migration to Babylonia as captives, prisoners, despoiled of their belongings, torn from their homeland and brought to barbarian lands, and there oppressed and treated as slaves in the harshest servitude.

Providence and divine mercy then ordered that in those times and in so calamitous a state there be many Prophets and many prophecies, some written in past times and others preached in the present, so that the people would not lose heart with the weight of their afflictions and, animated with the hope of freedom, could bear the travails of captivity. Captivity and the tyrant were oppressing them, the Prophets and the prophecies were giving them relief. The prophecies were sung to the sound of their chains and with the softness of this new sound the irons became less burdensome and the hearts stronger.

Most special among all the other Prophets was in this case the zeal and diligence of Jeremiah, for, having remained in Jerusalem where he suffered great hardships, imprisonments, and perils to his life for having preached and prophesied the truth (for which he finally died by stoning), in the midst of these oppressions and dangers to himself, not forgetful of those of others but, rather, quite mindful of what the exiles in Babylonia suffered, he wrote a book of his prophecies in which beforehand, in clear terms and words of great consolation, he foretold their freedom and the time of it, as can be seen in Chapter Twenty-Nine of this Prophet's words. The Prophet Baruch, Jeremiah's companion, brought this book to Babylonia and read it in the presence of King Jechonias and publicly to all people who lived with him in captivity; and this same Baruch notes how with

great excitement they all ran to the book. He says this in the first chapter of his account of this trip, which accompanies in the Holy Text the
works of Jeremiah: *Et legit Baruch verba libris hujus ad aures Jechoniae, filii
Joachim, regis Juda, et ad aures universi populi venientis ad librum.*[38]

I do not know if this book of ours of the *History of the Future* will have
the same good fortune and if it will be received and read with the same
animation and affection, but I do know that in the tribulations, calamities,
and afflictions that the World is to suffer, and which could reach Portugal
too, neither Portugal nor the World can have any other relief or any greater
consolation than the frequent lesson and consideration of this book and
the prophecies and promises of the future that will be seen written in it.
Portugal will not deny at least that in the time of its Babylonia and captivity and the oppressions during which so many times it has seen itself mis-
treated and put upon, there was no other appeal for its pain and no other
relief or consolation for its misery than the lesson and interpretation of the
prophecies and the hope of freedom and the year of it, and the length and
end of its captivity that were read in those pages.

It was read in the letter and tradition of Saint Bernard that if God at
some time allowed the kingdom to fall into the hands and power of a
foreign king, it would not be for a space of more than sixty years. It was
read in the oath of the King Afonso Henriques and in the promise of the
Hermit Saint that in the weakened sixteenth generation God would cast
his merciful eyes upon the Kingdom. It was read in the celebrated verses
of Bandarra that the desired time was to come, and hopes for it were to be
fulfilled in the year marked forty; and with the combination of all these
prophecies, Portugal was consoled and animated to go on living or lasting
until it saw their fulfillment.

Speaking of the same Babylonian captivity and of the relief and consolation his prophecies were to bring to those captives in their travails, the prophet
Isaiah states with both softness and eloquence these notable words: *Spiritus
Domini super me … ut mederer contritis corde et praedicarem captivis indulgentiam et … annum placabilem Domini … ut consolarer omnes lugentes … et
darem eis coronam pro cinere, oleum gaudii pro luctu.*[39] "The Lord descended
upon me and anointed me with his spirit," Isaiah says, "so that as a physician
of the afflicted captives of Babylonia, I might cure with the talent of my promises and prophecies, the sadness and faint-heartedness of their hearts." And
declaring more particularly the loving cures that he was applying to them, he
points out two that seem to be prescribed for our captivity rather than for
that of Babylonia: the first was a year of indulgence and redemption in which

the captivity was to end: *Et praedicarem captivitis indulgentiam, annum placabilem Domini;* the second was a crown in exchange for the ancient ashes, with which the mourning and past sadness would be converted into festivals and joy: *Et darem eis coronam pro cinere, oleum gaudii pro luctu.*

This is what Babylonian captives read in these prophecies and this is what we read in ours too. And just as they had no other cure for their grief but the hope of that longed for year and the change in that promised crown, so we too, with our eyes far off on the yearned for year forty and the hope for the crown of the new Portuguese king, were relieved from the weight of our yoke and consoled for the pain of our captivity. And since this cure of prophecies was so present and effective in past travails, I have good reason (and a reason based on experience) to hope and confirm that it will also be so for future things.

I do not promise nor do I expect misfortunes for Portugal. But if they be for Portugal, or for Christianity, or for the World, as might be caused by necessity or the adversity of the times, for all of them I offer this cure. It is better to have more cures with caution than to lack them improvidentially.

And for it not to seem that I am discussing only events and prophecies of ancient times, let the events and prophecies for our own times be written for them alone.

No one can ignore that the prophecies of the Book of Apocalypse (and especially those that remain to be fulfilled) belong to present times and will only stop with the end of the World. This is what the Fathers and Interpreters say and we shall bring it forth in its proper place. But to what end, I ask, did Divine Providence order for Saint John to have those revelations and write down those prophecies?

This question is the one whose answer was given to Saint Birgitta, as can be read in Book Six of her *Revelations.* With Christ wishing, as a particular favor, that the saint hear the answer from the Prophet himself, Saint John appeared to her and spoke thus: *Tu, Domine, inspirasti mihi mysteria ejus, et ego scripsi ad consolationem futurorum, ne fideles tui propter futurus casus everterentur.*[40] "You, Lord, revealed to me those mysteries, and I wrote the prophecies of them for the consolation of those to come and so that your faithful would not be perturbed with future events" but rather that they, confirmed by these same prophecies, would remain constant in their midst.

This is the reason (although not the only one) why God reveals future things and why the ancient Prophets and the last of them all, who was

Saint John, wrote them: so let it be seen how just and how useful, and how much in agreement with God's will and intent, is the diligence with which I have set myself to the task of choosing among all the prophecies those that pertain to our times, joining them all together, putting them in order, and bringing them to light for public benefit. And because the fruit of this benefit can be plucked from the news that this very year which we are entering promises to bring, applying the cure to the wound or to the threats of it, I say along with the prophet Amos: *Leo rugiet; quis non time-bit? Dominus Deus locutus est; quis non prophetabit?* [41] Is the Lion roaring? Yes, he is. Then now is the time for the prophecies to be heard and for it to be known and proclaimed what God has said: *Dominus Deus locutus est; quis non prophetabit?* Let all speak of prophecies and let all understand them, let all practice them, for now is the time.

When the roars of the Lion are heard in the sounds of his drums and trumpets, let there also be heard in our ears, and louder than all the other noises, the thunders of our prophecies. I call them this way because they are the voice of Heaven: *Leo rugiet, quis non timebit?* "When the lion roars, who will not tremble?" With reason will reply our soldiers that those who have defeated him so many times will not fear; that Portugal will not fear, for it is the Samson who so many times has broken the lion's jaw; that Portugal will not fear, for it is the Hercules who so many times has worn his skin; that Portugal will not fear, for it is the David who has saved his lambs from the lion's claws so many times. This is the reply of valor, but it can also be that of arrogance, with which God is not pleased.

Let not Portugal trust in itself so as not to offend God. Let it trust in God himself and in his promises, and it will fight with assurance. Oh! How well-armed will our soldiers be awaiting the Lion in the field if they have weapons in their hands and the prophecies in their heart! *Leo rugiet, quis non prophetabit?*

These are the trumpets of Heaven at whose sounds the walls of Jericho tremble and against whose battery no fortress can resist.

But if, perhaps, as might be the case, there were some adverse outcome (as after the miracle of Jericho there was in the field of Hai), let not Joshua or his soldiers lose their spirit; let them have recourse to God and his promises, with which for that reason he has forewarned us.

Divine Providence is accustomed to begin its miracles with opposite effects, either to test our faith or to raise its omnipotence even higher. It can do more than all human powers and there is only one thing it cannot do, which is to go back on what it has promised. Christ left the disciples to fight the storm on the first vigil, on the second he did not come to them, nor on the third; and when, on the fourth, after frightening them with phantoms, he succored them with his presence, even then he reprimanded them for their little faith. Let the night grow dark, let the sea roar, let the sky break forth, let the winds be furious, because God must come by his word. Secure is the Kingdom where it and the word of God run the same danger.

Notes
Anna M. Klobucka

In all quotes from the Bible, the New King James Version has been used as the primary source for English translations. Occasional minor adjustments have been made, both to the biblical text and to existing translations from other Latin sources, as required by Vieira's rhetorical use or adaptation of a given passage. Translations into English have been supplied whenever Vieira either does not offer his own or departs significantly from the original text.

References to Psalms in these notes are based on the Hebrew (Masoretic) system of numbering, which is used in the King James Bible and the Protestant tradition in general, and differs from the Greek (Septuagint) numbering used by Vieira.

Sermon of Saint Anthony to the Fish

[1] "You are the salt of the earth."

[2] "But if the salt loses its flavor, how shall it be seasoned? It is then good for nothing but to be thrown out and trampled underfoot by men" (Matthew 5:13).

[3] Matthew 13:47-48.

[4] "Let him have dominion over the fish of the sea, over the birds of the air, over the cattle and over all the earth" (Genesis 1:26).

[5] "God created great sea creatures" (Genesis 1:21).

[6] "Bless the Lord you whales and all that swim in the waters" (Daniel 3:79). From the "Song of Three Holy Youths," included in the Greek Septuagint and Roman Catholic and Eastern Orthodox versions of the Old Testament, but omitted from Protestant Bibles as apocryphal.

[7] "If you put a little piece of its heart upon coals, the smoke thereof drives away all kind of devils; and the gall is good for anointing the eyes, in which there is a white speck, and they shall be cured" (Tobit 6:8-9). The Book of Tobit (or Tobias) is considered apocryphal in the Protestant tradition.

[8] "Language is truly a small thing, but it conquers all with its might."

[9] James 3:3-4.

[10] Psalm 119:37.

[11] "Vanity of vanities, all is vanity" (Ecclesiastes 1:2).

[12] "The Spirit of God fertilized the waters." Vieira quotes here from what in another sermon ("Sermão de São Pedro" from 1644) he identifies and discusses as the "Hebrew original" of Genesis 1:2, distinct from the Vulgate verse *Spiritus Domini ferebatur super aquas* ("the Spirit of God was hovering over the face of the waters").

[13] Job 19:22. In his Portuguese translation of the biblical passage he quotes in Latin, Vieira expands and intensifies the wording of Job's outcry, a clearly intentional liberty that has been preserved here.

[14] "Have all the workers of iniquity no knowledge, who eat up my people as they eat bread?" (Psalm 14:4).

[15] "O ye, whom lord of land and waters wide / Of life and death grants here to have the pow'r, / Lay yer your proud and lofty looks aside: / What your inferior fears of you amiss, / That your superior threats to you again." Seneca, *Thyestes* ll. 607-611. English translation by Jasper Heywood (London: Ernest Benn & New York: W. W. Norton, 1982).

[16] Adapted by Vieira from St. Augustine's "Exposition of Psalm 38." St. Augustine's text, in an English translation by Maria Boulding, reads: "Take care that when you plan to prey on

smaller fry you do not become the prey of someone more powerful." *Expositions of the Psalms 33-50*, vol. III/16 of *The Works of Saint Augustine* (Hyde Park, NY: New City Press, 2000).

[17] Mark 14:37.

[18] "You know nothing at all" (John 11:49).

[19] "Do you not know that I have power?" (John 19:10).

[20] Matthew 2:20.

[21] "Now when Herod was dead ... those who sought the young Child's life are dead" (Matthew 2:19-20).

[22] "But it is good for me to draw near to God" (Psalm 73:28).

[23] John 18:8.

[24] "He who but a moment before had attempted to fly should not now be able to walk; and having affected wings should want the use of his heels." English translation by Joseph Blanco White, in *Practical and Internal Evidence Against Catholicism* (Cambridge: Manson and Grant/ Boston: William Peirce, 1835).

[25] Revelation 12:14.

[26] "Now a great sign appeared in heaven: a woman clothed with the sun" (Revelation 12:1).

[27] "[His canopy around Him was] dark waters and thick clouds of the skies" (Psalm 18:11).

[28] "It would have been good for that man if he had not been born" (Matthew 26:24). This is what Jesus says to his disciples of the man who will betray him (Judas).

Maundy Thursday Sermon

[1] "When Jesus knew that His hour had come that He should depart from this world to the Father, having loved His own who were in the world, He loved them to the end."

[2] John 13:3.

[3] John 13:11.

[4] John 13:7.

[5] John 1:12.

[6] "Lord, it is good for us to be here" (Matthew 17:4).

[7] John, 19:28.

[8] "Not knowing what he said" (Luke 9:33).

[9] "Knowing that all things were now accomplished, that the Scripture might be fulfilled, [Jesus] said, 'I thirst'" (John 19:28).

[10] "Knowing that His hour had come, He loved them to the end" (John 13:1).

[11] "Knowing that He had come from God" (John 13:3).

[12] "He knew who would betray Him" (John 13:11).

[13] "Having loved His own" (John 13:1).

[14] "[He] knew that His hour had come" (John 13:1).

[15] "O you whom my soul loves" (Song of Solomon 1:7).

[16] Song of Solomon 1:8.

[17] "Lord, are You washing my feet?" (John 13:6).

[18] "Knowing that the Father had given all things into His hands" (John 13:3).

[19] "[He] began to wash the disciples' feet" (John 13:5).

[20] "Take your sandals off your feet" (Exodus 3:5).

[21] "I am who I am" (Exodus 3:14).

[22] John 13:3-4.

[23] "Having loved His own who were in the world" (John 13:1).

[24] Sermon 83 on the Song of Songs.

[25] John 15:15.

[26] "Friend, why have you come?" (Matthew 26:50).

[27] "Then Jonathan and David made a covenant, because he loved him as his own soul" (1 Samuel 18:3).

[28] "Now Jonathan again caused David to vow, because he loved him" (1 Samuel 20:17).

[29] Genesis 22:2.

[30] "You have ravished my heart, / My sister, my spouse; / You have ravished my heart" (Song of Solomon 4:9).

[31] Psalm 104:19.

[32] John 18:4.

[33] "And having blindfolded Him, they struck Him on the face" (Luke 22:64).

[34] "Now I know that you fear God" (Genesis 22:12).

[35] "Now I know that you love God."

[36] Genesis 22:16-17.

[37] "Sustain me with cakes of raisins, / Refresh me with apples, / For I am lovesick" (Song of Solomon 2:5).

[38] Song of Solomon 5:8.

[39] Psalms 35:15. In the Latin text of the Clementine Vulgate the second clause of this sentence reads "et *ignoravi*" ("and *I* did not know it"); this version is also followed by all modern English translations of Psalm 35.

[40] "For He will be delivered to the Gentiles and will be mocked and insulted and spit upon. They will scourge Him and, after scourging, kill Him" (Luke 18: 32-33).

[41] "What I am doing you do not know" (John 13:7).

[42] Luke 23:34.

[43] Luke 2:7.

[44] John 21:15.

History of the Future

[1] "You will be like God, knowing good and evil" (Genesis 3:5).

[2] "Creatures of this class always deceive the ambitious, though those in power distrust them. Probably we shall go on for ever proscribing them and keeping them by us." Tacitus, *The Histories*, vol. I, 22. Trans. W. Hamilton Fyfe (Oxford: Clarendon Press, 1922).

[3] Vieira draws on and conflates two distinct sources here: Juvenal's mention of the silence of the oracle of Delphi in his sixth Satire ("Quoniam Delphis oracula cessant") and a passage from Book Five of Lucan's *Civil War* ("quam Delphica sedes / quod siluit, postquam reges timuere futura / et superos vetuere loqui"). However, his commentary appears to attribute the entire passage to Juvenal.

[4] "Your kingdom has been divided and given to the Medes and Persians" (Daniel 5:28).

[5] "Hope deferred makes the heart sick" (Proverbs 13:12).

[6] "Expect, expect again, / Expect, expect again, / Here a little, / There a little" (Isaiah 28:10).

[7] "Nor things instantaneous nor things to come" (Romans 8:38).

[8] "When the desire comes, it is a tree of life" (Proverbs 13:12).

[9] "[John the Baptist] was his herald and made him known when at last he came." From a prayer said at Mass during the Advent.

[10] "They called him Savior of the World in the Egyptian language" (Genesis 41:45). The Latin Vulgate version of this passage, quoted (and slightly paraphrased) by Vieira, differs from its rendition in Protestant Bibles, where Joseph's title is given as "Zaphenath-Paneah," an expression of uncertain meaning but often translated as "God speaks; he lives."

[11] Daniel 3:98 in the Vulgate; Daniel 4:1 in Protestant Bibles.

[12] "You … king … have grown and become strong; for your greatness … reaches to the heavens, and your dominion to the end of the earth" (Daniel 4:19 in the Vulgate; Daniel 4:22 in Protestant Bibles).

[13] "King Darius … to all peoples, nations, and languages that dwell in all the earth: Peace be multiplied to you" (Daniel 6:25). Vieira rephrases the passage to mirror more closely the description of Nebuchadnezzar he quotes above; the actual wording of the Latin text is: "Tunc Darius rex scripsit universis populis, tribubus, et linguis habitantibus in universa terra : Pax vobis multiplicetur."

[14] "Whereas I … had brought all the world under my dominion" (Esther 13:2 in the Clementine Vulgate). This passage belongs in one of the six chapters of the Book of Esther that originate in the Greek Septuagint. They do not appear in the Hebrew Bible and were not preserved in the Protestant tradition.

[15] "Now haughty Rome reigned mistress of the Globe, / Where'er the Ether shines with heavenly fires." Petronius, *Satyricon*, 119, 1-2. English translation by Alfred R. Allinson (New York: The Panurge Press, 1930).

[16] "There is no race which has not either been so utterly destroyed that it hardly exists, or so thoroughly subdued that it remains submissive, or so pacified that it rejoices in our victory and rule." Cicero, "De Provinciis Consularibus," xii, 31. English translation by R. Gardner in vol. XIII of the Loeb Classical Library edition of Cicero (Cambridge: Harvard University Press, 1958).

[17] "A decree went out from Caesar Augustus that all the world should be registered" (Luke 2:1).

[18] "He subdued Ocean to his governance and set the sky for border to his kingdom, ruling from Gades to the Tigris, and all that lies 'twixt Tanais and Nile." Claudian, *Panegyric on the Fourth Consulship of the Emperor Honorius*, 44-46. English translation by Maurice Platnauer in the Loeb Classical Library edition of Claudian (Cambridge: Harvard University Press, 1922).

[19] "The world was made through Him, and the world did not know Him" (John 1:10).

[20] Abraham Ortelius, *Theatrum Orbis Terrarum* (1570).

[21] "Due to fear or jealousy?" Tacitus, *The Annals*, Book I, 11. English translation by John Jackson in the Loeb Classical Library edition of *Annals* (Cambridge: Harvard University Press, 1925-1937).

[22] "[That they may …] know, and consider and understand … that the hand of the Lord has done this" (Isaiah 41:20).

[23] "As for this Moses, the man who brought us up out of the land of Egypt, we do not know what has become of him" (Exodus 32:1).

[24] "This is your god, O Israel, that brought you out of the land of Egypt!" (Exodus 32:4).

[25] "I have surely seen the oppression of My people who are in Egypt, and have heard their cry …. So I have come down to deliver them out of the hand of the Egyptians, and to bring them up from that land to a good and large land, to a land flowing with milk and honey" (Exodus 3:7-8).

[26] "How long will these people reject Me? And how long will they not believe Me, with all the signs which I have performed among them? … As I live (says the Lord), just as you have spoken in My hearing, so I will do to you. The carcasses of you [who have complained against

Me] shall fall in this wilderness; ... you shall by no means enter the land which I swore I would make you dwell in" (Numbers 14:11, 28-30).

27 "As you have spoken, so I will do to you" (Numbers 14:28).

28 "Out of your own mouth I will judge you" (Luke 19:22).

29 "As you have believed, so let it be done for you" (Matthew 8:13).

30 "Behold the proud, his soul is not upright in him; but the just shall live by his faith" (Habakkuk 2:4).

31 "If you will not believe, surely you shall not be established" (Isaiah 7:9).

32 "See, I have this day set you over the nations and over the kingdoms, to root out and to pull down, to destroy and to throw down, to build and to plant" (Jeremiah 1:10).

33 "Then He who sat on the throne said, 'Behold, I make all things new'" (Apocalypse 21:5).

34 "These words are true and faithful" (Apocalypse 21:5).

35 "Judgement will begin at the house of God" (1 Peter 4:17). The actual wording of this passage in the Clementine Vulgate is "Quoniam tempus est ut incipiat judicium a domo Dei" ("For the time has come for judgment to begin at the house of God").

36 "For whatever things were written before were written for our learning, that we through the patience and comfort of the Scriptures might have hope" (Romans 15:4).

37 "We, though we needed none of these things having for our comfort the holy books that are in our hands, chose rather to send to you to renew the brotherhood and friendship" (1 Maccabees 12:9-10). The Books of Maccabees are considered apocryphal in the Protestant tradition.

38 "And Baruch read the words of this book in the hearing of Jechonias the son of Joakim king of Juda, and in the hearing of all the people that came to hear the book" (Baruch 1:3). The Book of Baruch is considered apocryphal in the Protestant tradition. A somewhat different account of this reading is found in Jeremiah 36:10 ("Then Baruch read from the book the words of Jeremiah ... in the hearing of all the people").

39 "The Spirit of the Lord God is upon me ... He has sent me to heal the brokenhearted, to proclaim liberty to the captives ... to proclaim the acceptable year of the Lord ... to comfort all who mourn ... to give them a crown for ashes, the oil of joy for mourning" (Isaiah 61:1-3).

40 *Revelationes Sanctae Birgittae*, Book VI, Ch. 89.

41 "A lion has roared; who will not fear? The Lord God has spoken; who can but prophesy?" (Amos 3:8).